Before Summer

H. Arlo Nimmo

Prairie Avenue Productions
Chicago
2013

This book is a work of fiction.
All characters, places and events are creations
of the author's imagination.

© 2013 H. Arlo Nimmo. All rights reserved.

No part of this book may be reproduced or transmitted in any form
or by any means, electronic or mechanical, including photocopying
or recording, or by any information storage and retrieval system,
without permission in writing from the author.

Cover and book design by Cass Brayton
Cover photo © Shutterstock/Silver-John

Library of Congress Cataloging-in-Publication Data
Nimmo, Harry Arlo
Before Summer/ H. Arlo Nimmo
ISBN 978-1493637614
1. Gay fiction. 2. Rural Iowa. 3. 1940s and 1950s.
4. World War II. 5. College life.

To
my mother and father
and
my sisters and brothers
in
fond remembrance of those long ago
bittersweet days when we were all together.

Contents

Tools Rock 1

The Plum Tree 6

The War 22

God, Church and Jesus 34

Old Fred and Bucky 49

Miss Cotters 64

After the War 81

Minnie Wren 98

Bobbie, Gus and Winky 107

Ross 114

Mr. Fraser's Books 131

College 146

Rain 157

Wolf on the Prowl 169

Gunnar 183

Summer 198

. . . you are brilliant and subtle if you come from Iowa and really strange and you live as you live and you are always very well taken care of if you come from Iowa.

Gertrude Stein

Tools Rock

EXCEPT FOR THE missing apostrophe in our name and the big red rock in the corner of our Square, Tools Rock was like most of the other little towns scattered across the rolling prairies of central Iowa during the middle of the last century. The first white man to see the rock was Sebastian Tool who built his cabin beside it and immodestly named it for himself. His cabin soon became the center of a tiny hamlet as more settlers arrived to claim the surrounding land. When Tool officially founded the new town in 1846 and registered its name, he forgot the apostrophe, or more likely didn't know one was needed, and ever since we've taken a stubborn sort of pride in having no apostrophe in our name.

The rock is a puzzle. It stands alone and nothing resembles it until you reach the red rock bluffs of the Des Moines River about ten miles away. Roughly round in shape and about fifteen feet in diameter, its surface is covered with abstract incisions carved by Indians who once inhabited the area. Sebastian Tool added his name to the rock and throughout the years, townspeople—including a lot of my relatives—added theirs with dates and comments, creating a town registry etched in stone.

The first settlers of Tools Rock came from the eastern states after the land was confiscated from the Indians for white settlement. They brought their own brand of Methodism and built a church in a copse of oak trees while transforming the prairies into rich farmlands north and east of the new settlement. My great-grandparents came next with five other Scottish families who settled lands west of the emerging town. We Scots brought no church with us. I'm not sure why, but religion was never one of our needs. Marriages were always civil affairs and for years we conducted our own funerals and buried our dead in the cemetery on my grandparents' farm. The Dutch arrived next. Unhappy with the sin they perceived in Holland, they sought a wholesome place where they could practice their Calvinist religion without persecution. They discovered that place in the open prairies south of Tools Rock and their severe interpretation of the Bible eventually dominated the Baptist church. The three groups lived side by side for almost a century with little intermarriage. If we didn't marry someone within our own group, we found someone outside Tools Rock similar to ourselves. We liked one another well enough, but we simply preferred our own kind when it came to marriage.

At the center of town was the Square, or park, with its big red rock in the southwest corner. In the middle of the Square, a bandstand hosted weekly band concerts during the summer with special programs on Memorial Day, Fourth of July, Old Settlers' Day and Labor Day. Facing the Square on all sides, Victorian-façaded stores offered groceries, hardware, medicines, shoe repair, dry goods, farm equipment and other essentials to our little farming community. Competing to quench the town's thirst, two taverns unoriginally named the Southside Tavern and the Northside Tavern stared at one another from opposite sides of the Square and provided back alley entrances for those patrons wishing to avoid the censure of their teetotaling townsfolk. A block to the northwest, a grain elevator stored the farmers' harvests as they awaited transport to Chicago on steam-driven trains that stopped daily at the railroad depot. A redbrick schoolhouse, three blocks in the opposite direction, provided education for us kids.

The twelve hundred residents of Tools Rock lived in generic Iowa houses, some adorned with Victorian frills and wrap-around porches, radiating from the Square in all directions until halted by gently rolling farmlands that spread to the horizons like an embracing, undulating sea with occasional islands of self-sufficient farmsteads where many of my relatives lived with their menageries of farm animals. Rivers, roads and railroads meandered through the countryside, eventually reaching other small towns almost identical to Tools Rock.

The town harbored few secrets and no strangers. Everyone knew everyone else. Jenny Mason, our telephone operator, punctually sounded the noon whistle every day except Sunday and routinely listened to conversations, relaying discreetly edited versions to her family and friends. The school's sports events, class plays and music programs provided the town's most popular entertainment, but for us kids, summer was the most fun. In June, the Sun Players arrived with their big yellow tent and presented four nights of plays climaxed by a local talent show on Saturday night. In mid-July, the Fireman's Frolic, a three-day fundraiser for the volunteer fire department, featured a carnival in the Square complete with Ferris wheel, merry-go-round, amusement stands and "King Kong," an ageing wrestler who challenged our local stalwarts each year. The third weekend in August hosted Old Settler's Day, a homecoming celebration in the Square where local residents mingled with returning natives to the backdrop of a modest carnival. And periodically, a traveling evangelist arrived and erected a tent at the edge of town, tantalizing the locals with an alternative approach to God.

In spring, the freshly plowed fields surrounding Tools Rock filled the air with smells of primeval black earth. In early summer, those planted fields became squares of a gigantic quilt patterned in vibrant shades of green and trimmed with the roadside colors of wild flowers. Summer progressed with its sometimes awful heat, ripening crops and changing the quilt to tans, yellows and golds. During hot nights, fields crackled with the sounds of growing corn as the sweet fragrance of freshly mown hay hung heavily in the darkness. When summer gave way to fall, frosts added ambers and russets to the ever-changing countryside that sent explosions of color into the somber gray skies while scarlet sumac and orange bittersweet brightened the roadways. Flocks of geese and ducks honked and quacked their way southward through leaden skies, occasionally dipping into a farmer's pond for respite from their fatiguing flight. After autumn slipped away, the barren trees and empty fields patiently and quietly awaited the first snowfall. Then, gently and sometimes blizzardly, the land was transformed into stark whiteness, occasionally crystallized by devastating, but breathtakingly beautiful ice storms. Clusters of skeletal trees feigning death added dark splashes to the all-white world with occasional red barns standing out like exclamation points in the snowscape. Bitter, crackling cold held the countryside hostage throughout the long winter months. And then in mid-March, the winds and rains of spring returned, once again warming and wetting the fertile earth for rebirth, coaxing leaves and blossoms from awakening trees and sometimes overflowing creeks and rivers.

This was the Tools Rock of my youth.

The Plum Tree

"SHE SHOULD STAY home and get married before she's too old," muttered my Dad as he maneuvered our old Ford around a sharp turn in the muddy country road.

"But Letha wants an education, Ian," Mom replied.

"She went to high school, didn't she? That's enough education. No man'll want her if she's too educated."

Mom sighed and looked out the window. "She'll probably never come back to Tools Rock. She never belonged here. She always wanted to live in a big city."

Dad was silent for a moment and then said, "She'll come back when she fails."

It was the spring of 1940 and I was seven years old. I sat in the back seat with my sister Maggie who was four years younger. We were driving out to my grandparents' farm to see my aunt Letha who arrived the night before. I didn't like Dad talking that way about Letha. I hated it when anyone said bad things about her. Letha was my favorite aunt and I was so proud that she lived in Chicago and attended a university. No one else in my class had an aunt who lived in Chicago and attended a university.

I wasn't entirely sure what a university was but from what I heard, I was convinced it was good.

Dad cautiously steered the car along the slick road. Beyond the fences on either side, freshly plowed soil glistened blackly in the filtered sunlight of early spring. I liked the plowed fields. I liked the smell and I liked the sense of beginning when the dead winter fields were transformed into rich black promises. I knew the road by heart and looked forward to seeing my favorite scary places, the haunted house where a farmer was murdered years ago, the ditch where they found Grampa after he was stung by bees and the tree where old man Kline hanged himself. But today I was thinking so much about Letha that I didn't notice the house, the ditch or the tree. She sent me a letter and told me she was coming. It was the first time I ever received a letter. I showed it to some of my classmates at school, but I didn't let them read it.

Dad interrupted my thoughts. "She could've married any man she wanted. Seth Campbell was crazy about her. She'd been set with him. Old man Campbell owns half the county."

"But she's not ready to marry, Ian. I'm sure she'll find a good man when she's ready."

"All the good men'll be gone by the time she's ready."

"But education's good for a person." Mom sighed and looked out the window.

Dressed in black wool slacks and a dark green sweater, Letha was as pretty as I remembered. Gramma didn't approve of women wearing slacks, but she didn't say anything. We were sitting in the parlor at the farmhouse with Gramma and Grampa and Letha was telling us about the classes she was attending in Chicago. Mom was interested, but the others obviously weren't. Maggie was sleeping in the dining room on the daybed. I sat quietly and listened.

"How long will it take you to finish these classes?" asked Dad.

"At the rate I'm going, it'll take forever to finish my degree," laughed Letha. "But that's alright. I love going to school."

"Someday you've got to work."

"You're forgetting that I am working," Letha responded coolly. "I have a full-time job during the day and take classes at night."

"But you can't go to school all your life," said Gramma.

"Why not? It's better than the way most people spend their lives."

"I'm sure Letha will finish school someday and make us all proud of her," said Mom.

The others said nothing.

"You've hardly spoken, Lach," said Letha. She smiled at me. "How'd you like to take a walk with me? I haven't been outdoors since I arrived."

"It's awfully muddy out, Letha," said Gramma. "You'll ruin your shoes."

"I'll put on Dad's boots and Lach has his overshoes. Do you want to come, Lach?"

I smiled and nodded my head eagerly.

"Be careful, Letha. And don't go too far," cautioned Gramma.

We went to the back porch where Letha put on Grampa's oversized boots and I buckled up my overshoes. Outdoor, a steel gray sky obscured the sun.

"It's so good to be out of that house," Letha said, stretching her arms above her head. "Sometimes I feel like I'm suffocating in there. Take my hand, Lach." She held out her hand and I shyly took it. "You're the only one I miss when I'm away. I wish I could take you back to Chicago with me. How would you like that?"

"I'd love to see Chicago, but I'd probably get homesick. I get homesick when I stay away from home." We walked toward the barnyard.

"But I'd be there and we'd have a great time. When you're older, I'll send you a ticket and you can take the train to Chicago all by yourself and I'll meet you at the station. I'll show you so many wonderful things. We'll go to the museum and the library. And we'll see a play. And the stockyards. They're so huge, so many pigs and cattle. And wait until you see how big the lake is."

"I'd really like that," I said, excitedly. I'd never been on a train before. In fact, I was a little afraid of the noisy, hissing steam engines that stopped at the depot in Tools Rock.

"Let's go to Calhoun Creek and look for tadpoles," suggested Letha. We entered the barnyard and I threw corncobs to scare away pigs before we opened the gate to the pasture. We walked across the spongy grass and followed the path downhill to the creek, stepping around cow patties.

"There should be a log down that bank where we can sit," said Letha, scanning the creek. "There it is."

We scrambled down the creek bank and sat on the log.

"This was my favorite place when I was little. Sometimes I'd come here and hide from the others." She looked into the creek. "Do you see any tadpoles?"

"I don't see any." I peered into the water.

"Maybe it's too early. If you come back in a couple of weeks there'll be some." She picked up a stick and stirred the water. "What are you studying in school?"

"The same old stuff." I found a stick and poked it into the soft creek bed.

"What classes do you like best?"

I thought a minute. "I really like reading a lot—if the stories are good. But some of them are boring. Sometimes we have to read out loud and some of the kids can't read too good. I like geography too. Last week we read about China. Someday I'd like to go to China, but I probably never will."

"Why not?"

I shrugged and threw my stick across the creek.

"You can go anywhere and do anything you want, Lach. Don't let anyone tell you differently."

"But it costs a lot of money, and I don't have any money."

"If you really want to go, you'll find a way."

"I really want to go," I said excitedly. "I want to travel everywhere in the world."

Letha looked at me quietly and said, "You can do it, Lach. I got away from Tools Rock, and you can too. We're a lot alike. We look alike. We have black hair. The rest of the family has that yucky red hair. We have green eyes. The others have those boring blue eyes. You're going to be tall like me too. But most important you have my spirit. You won't be content to stay here. And I'll help you get away. You can do great things with your life."

"Do you think so?" I asked, excited at the prospect of an adventuresome life.

"I know so." Letha stood. "Come. I want to show you something. Maybe it's too early." We followed the winding creek.

"It should be right around this next bend."

We followed the bend and stopped. Before us a plum tree was in spectacular bloom. It spread over the creek, its snowy branches reflected in a quiet pool where the streambed widened. It stood ghost-like, against the gray sky and bleak early spring countryside. Petals drifted to the water and the slow current carried them lazily downstream. Transfixed by its beauty, I quietly gazed at it.

"This is my own special plum tree," said Letha. "I discovered it years ago and every spring when I'm home I come down here to see it. Let's sit beneath it and let the blossoms fall on us."

She took me by the hand and led me to a big rock beneath the tree where we sat side by side. The hum of bees among the blossoms and the quiet ripple of the water moving around three large stones provided the only sounds. Falling petals stuck in our hair and on our clothes.

"Isn't it beautiful?" said Letha. She pulled me to her and kissed my forehead. I hugged her back. I loved Letha. "It's our special place, Lach. I came here all by myself when I was little and dreamt about all the wonderful things I would do someday. It's an enchanted place. It will always be part of me. When you visit the farm, you can come here and be near me because part of me will always be here.

It can be your special place, too, where you can dream any kind of dream and nobody will laugh at you."

We sat quietly side by side, the falling blossoms clinging to us. Letha suddenly leaned forward, peered into the water, and said, "Look! Tadpoles!" I joined her and saw tiny tadpoles wiggling through the water.

"Now it's complete," she said.

It was Thanksgiving and my grandparents' farmhouse was packed with aunts and uncles and cousins—and Letha, who arrived the previous day. We had stuffed ourselves on pheasants and roast chicken. Sage dressing, mashed potatoes, escalloped corn, gravy, and mincemeat pie rounded out the dinner. The women were clearing up the remains of the meal while the men digested their portions in the parlor. I was outdoors in the yard with two cousins I didn't like much. I'd rather be indoors with the adults, but my cousins wanted to play and Mom urged me to join them.

"Let's go down to the barn and I'll show you how to smoke," said Davie.

"Okay," said James. The younger boy followed the older one through the gate.

"You coming, Lach?"

"I don't wanna smoke."

"Suit yourself. You never wanna do anything."

The boys disappeared behind the garage.

I sat on the steps of the wash house and stroked the white cat stretched lazily at my feet in the warm afternoon sun. Letha once told me the old wash house was the first house my great-grandparents built when they arrived from Scotland and settled the land. It was hard to believe they lived in the little one-room house with five kids. It was bad enough that I had to share a bedroom with my older brother Duncan. Nearby a half-dozen chickens clucked contentedly as they scratched for their own Thanksgiving morsels.

The kitchen door opened and Letha appeared. She was dressed in overalls and a denim shirt, but she still looked beautiful. She joined me on the steps.

"Where are the other boys?"

"Playing down by the barn."

"Why aren't you with them?"

"They always do dumb things."

Letha stood. "Come. Let's go down to the creek and see our plum tree."

We walked hand-in-hand through the barnyard, climbed over the fence to the pasture and followed a cow path toward the creek. Letha stopped at a salt block.

"Do you ever lick the salt block?" she asked me.

I shook my head. "Mom says it's dirty."

"It's okay if you clean a place on the side where the cows haven't licked." She knelt at the block and rubbed its side until it was clean. She leaned over and licked it. "Try it."

I leaned over and cautiously licked at the spot. I made a face and stuck out my tongue. "It's really salty."

"Of course, it is," laughed Letha. "That's why the cows like it. I'll race you to the creek."

She ran across the pasture with me directly behind her. She scrambled down the bank and sat on the big rock beneath the plum tree. I sat beside her.

"Our tadpoles have turned into frogs and are buried in the mud waiting for spring," she said, studying the leaf-choked creek. "And look at the poor plum tree. It looks dead, but it isn't. Next spring it'll be beautiful again. Nothing really dies. It always comes back as part of life again. Living on a farm teaches you that, Lach. Things seem to die, but they really don't. They're always reborn. City people don't understand that."

"But I thought you didn't like the farm. Isn't that why you went to Chicago?"

"Oh no, Lach. I love the farm. That's why I come back. I'll always come back."

"But why don't you stay here? Why do you have to go back to Chicago?"

"It's the people, Lach. I like the city people. They think like I do. I don't feel so lonely there. I love my family, but I'm not like them. Something made me different from them, Lach. As much as I love the farm, I'm not happy here. Someday you'll understand what I mean."

She stood. "Come, I want to show you a special place."

She led me upstream until we reached a curve where the creek bed widened. She approached a low bank, leaned over and examined it carefully. "Sometimes I find arrowheads and pieces of pottery here. This used to be an Indian campsite."

I was excited. "You mean Indians used to live here? How do you know?"

"I found lots of pottery and arrowheads here. Look. Here's a piece of pottery." She pulled a small shard from the bank and handed it to me.

"A real Indian made this?" I asked, examining the shard closely.

"Several Indian families probably lived here before our family came along. Uncle Adam told me about the Indians who lived here when he was little."

"Wow! I never knew Indians lived here. That's so great." I looked around at the site. "What a great place to live."

"Indians lived on all this land before the white people came and took it from them. I'm taking a class about Indians."

"I'd love a class about Indians. We never study anything good like that."

"You will when you go to the university."

"Do you think I'll go to the university?"

"Yes, you will, Lach. I'm sure you will." She looked at me quietly and then said, "Let's go see the old cabin where Uncle Adam was born. I think it's still standing."

I wrote to Letha almost every week after she returned to Chicago. I felt so adult when I took my letter to the post office and asked for a stamp that would deliver it to Chicago. And the days were so special when I returned home from school and found one of her letters awaiting me. I never let anyone read them, but sometimes I read passages to my good friends. Letha told me about her exciting life in Chicago. I first heard about operas and symphonies from her. She told me about a big St. Patrick's Day parade she attended. The only parade I'd ever seen was our high school parade before the homecoming football game. Once she went sailing on the lake. I knew about lakes, but I wasn't sure about sailing them. The only sailboats I heard about were the ones like Columbus had. She promised me I'd see all those things when I visited her in Chicago. At night before I slept, I sometimes fantasized about exploring that exciting wonderful world of Chicago with my beautiful aunt.

It was almost ten o'clock on a Friday night in late April and because there was no school the next day, I wasn't in bed yet. I was in the kitchen with Mom and Dad when the telephone rang. They looked at one another apprehensively. No one ever called so late. Mom cautiously lifted the receiver from the old oak wall-phone and said, "Hello." Then she said, "Yes, it is." And then, "Yes, he is." She turned to Dad and said, "It's from Chicago. They want to talk to you." She was frightened.

Dad took the receiver and said, "Hello. Yes, this is Ian MacLennan." He listened quietly for several moments. Then his face changed. I'd never seen him look like that. He turned ashen and his mouth opened. His voice cracked when he said, "Thanks for calling." He replaced the receiver and dropped into the chair, staring blankly.

"What is it, Ian?" asked Mom.

Dad said nothing.

"What is it? What happened?"

He stared at her for several moments and then said, "Letha's dead."

The coffin was in the living room. I'd hardly spoken or eaten since we received that telephone call. The coffin arrived at the train station in Carston where we always met Letha when she came from Chicago. For two days heavy rain fell and we were unable to take Letha's body to the farm where the funeral service would be held before burial in the family cemetery. The rain finally stopped. The next day a hearse would transport the coffin to the end of the gravel road where it would be transferred to a wagon that a team of horses would pull over the slick muddy road to the farmhouse.

It was still drizzling light rain the next morning but the sun was breaking through the gray clouds. Duncan and I rode in the old Ford with Dad behind the hearse to the end of the gravel road where Grampa was waiting with the farm wagon and horses. The undertaker helped transfer the coffin to the wagon and then left after offering some sympathetic platitudes. I sat between Dad and Grampa on the hard wagon seat. Duncan found a place beside the coffin in the back.

"Awful weather for May," said Grampa. "Everyone's way behind on plowing."

"How's Mother?" asked Dad.

"She's holding up. Keeps saying we shouldn't have let Letha go to Chicago. This wouldn't have happened."

"She was determined to leave. You couldn't have kept her here."

"That's what I keep telling her. But you know your mother. Always blaming herself."

"Letha was a stubborn woman. When she was here last fall, she told me she had kidney stones but she was determined to finish her classes before she had an operation. Foolish woman."

"She did what she had to do," said Grampa. "That's all any of us can do."

Suddenly one of the horses slipped and lurched, pulling the other horse and the wagon into the ditch. The coffin slid part way off the wagon into the muddy bank. I was terrified, irrationally thinking Letha might be hurt. I started to cry. Grampa scurried from his seat to check the horses. They were uninjured.

"Stop crying, Lach," said Dad. "There's nothing to be gained by that."

"Let the boy cry, Ian. He was awfully fond of Letha. And he was her favorite."

The men shoved the coffin back onto the wagon and we resumed our journey. I stifled my tears, but continued to hurt inside.

"Don't tell your mother about that," said Grampa. "She'll think it's a bad omen."

"Nothing but muddy roads."

We reached the farmhouse. Gramma and Aunt Grace came from the house as we pulled into the yard.

"Where'd all the mud come from?" asked Gramma when she saw the coffin.

"There's mud everywhere," said Grampa. "Better get a rag and clean it before we take it inside."

Aunt Grace went into the house and returned a few minutes later with a bucket of water and some rags. The women cleaned the coffin while we quietly watched. The men then carried it into the house and placed it in front of the big parlor window that looked onto empty plowed fields.

"Alexander called. He said he'd be happy to say a few

words before the burial," said Gramma. She hesitated. "Mary called too. She thought maybe we should have a minister come out."

"We know how to bury our own dead," said Grampa.

"She thought it might look better."

"We'll do it the way we've always done it."

Gramma lit a kerosene lamp and placed it on a table near the coffin. The others went to the kitchen for coffee and sandwiches. I sat in the parlor on the old horsehair sofa, still wearing my hat and coat, staring at the coffin.

"Don't you want something to eat, Lachlan?" asked Gramma.

I shook my head and she left the room. I sat in the dark room, hurting inside like I'd never hurt before. I understood that Letha was dead; I knew what "dead" was. I'd seen plenty of dead animals on the farm. But I didn't know why I was hurting so much. I didn't understand the pain inside me. I knew what hurt was like when I got sick and threw-up or when I stubbed my toe or hit my thumb with a hammer or when I got my finger caught in the car door. But that was nothing like this hurt. Maybe I was going to die too. I stared at the coffin.

In the early afternoon, relatives began arriving. Dad and my uncle Gavin took turns driving the horses and wagon back and forth from the gravel road to pick them up. Several kids arrived, but I wasn't interested in playing with them and stayed in the parlor on the sofa. That night all the beds in the house were filled and I had to share the sofa in the parlor with a cousin I didn't know.

❧   ❧   ❧

Dawn ushered in the first warm day of spring and the sun shone brightly. I was shooed from the parlor by my aunts so they could prepare it for the funeral service. Someone brought two bouquets of flowers from Des Moines and placed them at either end of the coffin. An early lunch was served and the mourners took their plates outdoors to enjoy the warm weather. Mom gave me a chicken sandwich and a piece of cake and insisted I eat as she watched. After lunch, my parents went inside to open the coffin. Dad undid the screws and when the lid was opened, Mom adjusted Letha's body. She then sat beside me on the sofa as mourners passed the coffin.

Most looked quietly at the body a few moments and then moved on. Some of the women murmured sadly and dabbed moist eyes with fancy little handkerchiefs. Their men stood beside them, awkward and stony-faced.

"She looks so natural," murmured Aunt Blanche, sniffing into her lavender handkerchief.

"So young and so pretty," sighed a neighboring farmwife. "Such a terrible shame."

Mom whispered to me, "You can see Letha now, Lach."

I slipped off the sofa and slowly walked toward the coffin, keeping my eyes on the floor. When I reached the coffin, I reluctantly raised my eyes to the corpse. I gasped. It wasn't Letha! It didn't look like Letha! It looked like a dummy in the Sears Roebuck window at Carston. It had no color. There was no smile. Something was wrong. Letha wasn't there. Someone made a mistake. I turned and hurried from the room. Mom followed me.

"Lach! What is it? Come back!"

I ran from the house and crossed the yard. I climbed over the gate and raced through the barnyard scattering pigs and chickens. I scurried over the fence to the pasture and slipped in a mud puddle.

"Lach! Lach!" Mom called from the yard.

I sprinted across the pasture, tripping over tangled weeds. When I reached the creek, I was covered with mud. I slid down the bank, ran past the log where Letha and I searched for tadpoles and hurried around the bend. Suddenly I stopped.

The plum tree towered above me. Its blossom-studded branches sparkled whitely in the spring sunshine against the brilliant blue sky. I stared at it, momentarily mesmerized by its beauty. I ran beneath its branches, skipping and laughing, holding up my hands and catching the falling petals. I twirled and danced around the tree until I stumbled and fell to the ground, the drifting petals slowly and quietly covering me.

"She's alive!" I shouted. "She's not dead! She's alive! She's alive!"

The War

ALWAYS FELT A little guilty because I had so much fun during World War II. Despite the horrors of those awful years, it remains in my childhood memory as a mosaic of exciting adventures and good times. I remember when it began. My sister Maggie and I were playing in the backyard on a warm December Sunday afternoon.

Miss Cotters, our neighbor, appeared at her back door and called across the garden, "Did your parents hear the news?"

"What news?" I asked.

"The Japs bombed us. You better tell them. Everyone's talking about it."

Maggie and I ran into the kitchen and relayed the news to Mom. She hurried to the living room where Dad was reading a newspaper. They turned on the radio and found a station reporting the Japanese attack on Pearl Harbor. I didn't understand most of what was said, but I knew it was serious because each time I asked a question I was shushed. We huddled around the radio the entire afternoon.

THE WAR

Just before supper, my older brother Duncan rushed into the house and announced, "Everyone uptown is talking about the sneaky Japs. Bob Johnson's joining the army so he can fight them."

"When's he going?" I asked.

"As soon as he can. I wish I was old enough to go before they bomb Tools Rock."

"Where's Pearl Harbor?" I asked. "When are they going to bomb us?" I was terrified.

"Pearl Harbor's in Hawaii way out in the middle of the Pacific Ocean," said Mom. "The Japanese aren't going to bomb Tools Rock."

We continued listening to the radio but I lost interest when I learned Pearl Harbor was thousands of miles away and the Japs probably wouldn't be dropping any bombs on us. After supper, the rest of the family listened to the radio, but I took my favorite *National Geographic* magazines to the kitchen. It was nice having the room to myself.

Everyone talked about the war during the next few weeks, but I lost interest in it until I came home from school one afternoon and found Mom crying. It always scared me when Mom cried. She told me that Dad's youngest brother had joined the Army Air Corps and she was afraid something would happen to him. Her oldest brother was killed in the Great War and she always said she hated wars. Grant was my favorite uncle and I didn't want him killed in the war. Two weeks later he left for the war and I hugged him goodbye. When he returned home four years later, I was too old to be hugged. Grant was different anyway so it didn't matter.

Several weeks after Grant left, Mom and Dad began serious discussions sometimes lasting late into the night, long beyond their normal bedtime. Papers arrived through the mail and they studied them carefully. I eventually learned that Dad had applied for a wartime job. The war needed civilian workers and the government was offering good salaries. Iowa was still emerging from the Depression, and after years of struggling to make enough money to feed us, Dad, like many others, was attracted to the high-paying defense jobs.

Dad was assigned to Pine Camp, an army base in upstate New York. Duncan hoped we'd go to California where he might see some movie stars and was disappointed when he learned we were going to New York. But I didn't care. I was excited at the prospect of going anywhere. After school ended, packing crates arrived and everything was chaotic for the next two weeks as we packed our possessions. A truck came, loaded the crates and took them to the railroad depot where they were shipped to New York. That night we slept at the farm. Early the next morning, after a big breakfast, we were ready to begin our journey. Mom and Gramma hugged and cried. We settled into the 1938 Pontiac sedan Dad bought for the trip and drove away as Mom continued crying. Maggie cried too, but she didn't know what she was crying about. I was happy we were leaving, but I didn't let anyone know and pretended I was sad.

We drove straight through to New York, stopping only a few hours each night when Dad couldn't stay awake any longer. The beginning of the trip was exciting as we traveled through places I'd never seen before. I played games

THE WAR

with Maggie, like counting cows and horses. I always chose cows because there were more of them and I liked to win. The Burma Shave signs were funny at first, but I grew tired of them. We stopped at restaurants for hamburgers. Sometimes we stopped at a grocery store along the highway and Mom made lunch for us. I read the comic books several times. Rains provided occasional diversions, but overall travel wasn't as exciting as I thought it would be.

As we got further away from Iowa, the people looked different. A lot of them had black hair. They talked funny, too. We saw four Negro men on a street corner in Cleveland. I'd only seen Negroes in pictures and was amazed at how dark they were. One of them wore a bright red shirt and a matching hat. I thought I saw a Jap at a gas station in Pennsylvania, but the attendant said he was a Chinese. I didn't know they looked so much alike. Mom and Dad talked about the changing countryside, but it all looked the same to me until we reached upstate New York where cultivated fields gave way to rocky hills and forests. I wondered if Indians lived in the forests. When we reached Pine Camp, we learned our furniture hadn't arrived, so we stayed at a tourist camp. Duncan and I slept in one of the little houses. It had its own radio, but since Duncan was five years older than me, he always decided what station we heard.

I loved Pine Camp the minute we arrived. Soldiers were everywhere. We lived in the civilian housing quarters at the edge of the camp. I made friends easily and soon knew all the neighborhood kids who came from all over the U. S. Some of them talked weird, especially a boy from

BEFORE SUMMER

New York City. Joey Wells impressed me most. He was at Pearl Harbor when the Japs attacked and told scary stories about exploding bombs and people getting killed. His parents were divorced and I felt sorry for him because he didn't have a dad around, but I soon discovered a lot of dads weren't around.

Behind our house was a forest. We kids played there, but we were warned to stay away from the river that ran through it. We didn't, of course. We soon knew every curve and cranny of the river as well as the abandoned houses scattered along its banks. We initially avoided them, thinking they might be haunted, but we eventually ventured into one that became headquarters for our secret club. When winter came, snow reached our roof and banished certain sections of the forest until spring.

The army base was our playground. The soldiers frequently invited us kids into the military facilities. At the gym we befriended a redheaded boxer who sparred and wrestled with us. I rolled on the mat with him, felt his strong body and rubbed the coarse hair on his chest. A burly soldier from Minnesota gave us rides in a tank and sometimes knocked down trees. At the service club, a chubby Italian manager from Brooklyn treated us to ice cream cones.

We routinely visited the base hospital. It was a one-story building that stretched along the route we walked during our explorations. When winter arrived, we discovered we could enter the hospital's back entrance and walk its halls to the front, thereby avoiding a long walk in the cold. Sometimes it took us a couple of hours to walk through the hospital as we stopped and talked to all the

THE WAR

patients we befriended. Some of them were amputees, some were blind and others were bandaged with wounds I didn't understand. At first, the nurses ordered us out, but they eventually realized we were good morale-boosters for the patients and allowed us to stay. One Christmas, the hospital hosted a party for us kids and a patient dressed as Santa Claus distributed gifts. But the most fun part was when three GIs pretended they were the Andrews Sisters, wearing kerchiefs, make-up, and stuffed T-shirts, as they sang "Shoo-Shoo Baby."

During the summer, we collected pop and beer bottles along the roads and redeemed them for two cents apiece. Joey Wells and I once made three dollars. We stuffed ourselves on ice cream and candy, and then treated the other kids. We still had enough money to buy two packs of cigarettes in the nearby town at the little store owned by an old couple who never challenged us when we said the cigarettes were for our parents. Camels were my favorites because of the picture on the package. But I didn't care much for smoking and usually gave my cigarettes to the other boys. One day while playing behind a barracks, we found a bag of stolen mail. We reported it to the MPs and later received a letter of commendation from the base commander.

I saw my first movie at Pine Camp. It was in Technicolor with Carmen Miranda wearing brightly colored South American clothes, thick-soled shoes and tall hats filled with fruit. I went to the movies two or three times a week at the base theater where admission was only a nickel. My friends and I stood in the long lines with the GIs who sometimes picked us up and passed us from soldier-to-soldier to the front of the line. I liked the touch and smell of the soldiers, as well as the candy bars they sometimes gave us.

I loved the music of the war. My favorite singers were the Andrews Sisters and I saw all their movies. Duncan said they were homely. Maybe they were, but they certainly knew how to sing happy songs. Once they visited Pine Camp with a USO show and I saw them perform. I was thrilled. It was my first time to see famous people.

I was about eleven or twelve when I sensed that my feelings toward the GIs were sexual. I liked their touch when I romped with them in the gym. The feel of the hair on their chests and arms aroused me in ways I didn't understand. I liked it when they picked me up at the movie theater and passed me to the front of the line. And when I saw several of them showering at the gym, something warm and exciting welled within me.

Buzzy Randall was fat and a little retarded and none of the other kids wanted to play with him. I felt sorry for him because he didn't have any friends so I sometimes played with him. One day I invited him to our secret cave at the river and gave him a cigarette. He inhaled without choking, something I couldn't do.

"You really know how to smoke," I said, admiringly.

"Yeah, my friend Stan taught me." Buzzy blew a smoke ring. I was impressed.

"Who's Stan?" I didn't know any Stan among the Pine Camp kids.

"He's a guard at the Great Bend Gate. He shows me his peter." Buzzy blew another smoke ring.

"He shows you his peter?"

"Yeah. You wanna see him?"

"Maybe," I said cautiously.

"Let's go over to the gate," suggested Buzzy. "Maybe Stan's there."

We kids knew all the guards at the entrances to Pine Camp. The Great Bend gate never had much traffic, so we often hung out there and talked to the soldiers. I didn't know any guard named Stan, but Buzzy obviously did.

We walked through the forest to the gate and discovered a new guard on duty.

"Where's Stan?" asked Buzzy.

"You won't be seeing Stan anymore," said the new guard, waving us through the gate.

I later learned that Buzzy told others about his encounters with Stan and he was arrested. We never heard of him again. Nor did we hear again of the scoutmaster who invited older boys to his house to talk about their peters. I soon learned that the feelings and thoughts that gave me such warm pleasure couldn't be shared with anyone.

We kids from Pine Camp attended school in a nearby little town. Each morning a bus transported us to school and returned us in the afternoon. Friday was Bond Day and I took my dimes to school and bought stamps that I pasted into my savings book. At some future date, I would have enough stamps to buy a bond. I took great pride in adding each stamp to my book, carefully placing it in its proper square. I knew that somehow I was helping defeat the Krauts and Japs. I also collected cellophane, tin foil and string which I took to school and added to the other kids' collections. I wasn't sure why we collected them, but the teacher said they would help win the war. One fall I collected the downy seedpods of milkweeds which my teacher said would be used in a lifejacket for some soldier, sailor or marine. I felt good knowing I was saving someone's life.

Although I was told they were make-believe, the air raid drills scared me, especially the ones at night. When the siren sounded and the lights turned off, we waited in the dark for the all-clear siren. I preferred sitting near Mom and Dad during the blackouts, but sometimes Maggie and I crawled behind the couch and huddled together until the lights came on. At school we were ushered into the basement until the all-clear signal sounded. The teacher always told us it was a practice drill, but I never knew when one might be real. I saw movies of air raids with bombs screeching through the sky exploding buildings and killing people. Mom said we lived too far away from the battlegrounds to be concerned about real air raids. But I wasn't sure. Why did we have air raid drills if there wasn't any danger?

I saw my first Negroes up-close at Pine Camp. A regiment of Negro soldiers was stationed on the base, but they were segregated from the white soldiers, so I didn't see too much of them. One day when Joey and I were playing in the forest, we saw a tall Negro soldier and a Negro woman walking along the river. We followed them, keeping to the forest so we wouldn't be seen. They found a small clearing, spread a blanket and lay on it smoking cigarettes and talking. We were close enough to hear their conversation.

"Is Dad still working those long hours at the plant?" the man asked.

"Yes. Sometimes he does double shifts," said the woman. "He's hoping he can save enough money to buy a house. He says if that happens, at least one good thing will come from this war."

"How about Mom?"

"She still gets awfully tired but she's getting better. It'll take a while."

They talked sorta funny, but what they talked about seemed the same thing most older people talked about. We soon decided Negroes weren't all that different from other people, except for their color.

During my third year at Pine Camp, German prisoners arrived. Joey and I learned where they were quartered. We sat on a small hill some distance from the enclosure and watched them, afraid to get too close. Later, German prisoners accompanied by guards collected our garbage and mowed our lawn. One day I was sitting on the porch when two prisoners arrived to mow. I usually hurried away when I saw prisoners, but a guard was with these two so I decided to stay and watch them. One of them, a tall blond man who didn't look too old, came over to the porch to pull weeds. Up close, he looked like an American. I was amazed at how normal he seemed.

"Hello," he said.

I was surprised and a little scared, but I said, "Hello."

"My name is Max. What's your name?"

He had a weird way of talking, but I could understand him. "Lach," I said.

"That's a nice name."

"Thank you."

"Would you like a candy bar?"

Always ready for a candy bar, I said, "Yes."

He pulled a Milky Way from his shirt pocket and handed it to me.

"Thank you."

"I must work now," he said.

"Okay."

He began pulling weeds and I went into the house where Mom was peeling potatoes in the kitchen. "Look what the German prisoner gave me," I said, handing her the candy bar. "Do you think it's poisoned?"

Mom looked at the candy bar carefully and said "Why do you think it would be poisoned?"

"Germans hate us and he might want to kill me."

"Not all Germans hate us," she smiled, returning the candy bar. "I'm sure many of them dislike this war as much as we do. You probably reminded the prisoner of his little brother or maybe his son."

I felt differently about Germans after that, but it was several days before I ate the Milky Way.

Italian prisoners arrived at the camp too. I liked the musical sounds of their language. Some of them worked as pinsetters at the camp's bowling alley. Once when a neighbor woman and her girlfriends were bowling, the prisoners sent them notes written in Italian tucked into the thumbholes of the bowling balls. When she showed her note to Mom I said I wished I understood the writing. Mom said it was probably just as well that I didn't.

THE WAR

And then as quickly as it began, the war ended. I knew we'd beaten the Germans but I didn't think we'd beat the Japs so soon. A big bomb was dropped on Japan and that was the end of the war.

We lived in New York three years. I didn't realize that after the war we would return to Tools Rock, but that's what happened.

God, Church and Jesus

IN LATE JUNE, one of my seventh grade classmates hosted a party at her home in the country a few miles outside Tools Rock. It was already a hot summer and June was promising to break all heat records. Day after day, ninety and hundred-degree temperatures exhausted everyone. Only the corn thrived and farmers predicted record-breaking crops.

I wasn't enthusiastic about the party. Some of my least favorite classmates were there and the hosts were Dutch fundamentalist Baptists, a combination that put a damper on most things I liked. Following a big farm supper of fried chicken, mashed potatoes, green beans, corn-on-the-cob and homemade ice cream, it was time to go home. We piled into Mr. Van Dyk's Buick for the ride back to Tools Rock. Half-way to town, the car hit loose gravel, swerved and ended up in a ditch. No one was injured but a tow was needed to retrieve the car. Mr. Van Dyk walked to a nearby farmhouse for help while we kids remained in the car.

As we settled into the wait, Willadean Van Dyk announced, "God was with us."

Velma Vander Zee added, "I began praying when we hit the gravel. I'm so glad I'm saved. My brother was baptized last Sunday. Now all my family will be together in heaven."

"My family's all saved, too," announced Cornie Van de Wilt.

I had no idea what they were talking about and said, "What do you mean 'saved'? Who saved you?"

"We've been baptized. We've accepted Jesus Christ as our savior. Our sins are washed away and we'll enter the kingdom of heaven," explained Jake de Mier.

"What sins?" I asked.

"The sins we're born with. Everyone's born in sin. It's only after you accept Jesus and are baptized that you're cleansed of your sins. Then you must always lead a clean life so you can join Jesus in heaven."

"Aren't you baptized, Lach?"

They all looked at me expectantly. I was momentarily quiet and then said, "I don't think so."

Velma gasped. Jake said, "You'd know if you were."

"I'll pray for you," said Willadean.

"What are you going to pray about?"

"I'll pray that you accept Jesus Christ into your life so you'll be saved and not burn in Hell."

"Why would I burn in Hell?"

"Punishment for your sins," explained Jake, patiently.

"But what did I do?"

"You were born in sin and you haven't been saved."

"You mean even though I didn't do anything I'm going to Hell?"

"You're a sinner," persisted Willadean. "And Hell is a horrible place. You wouldn't believe what happens in Hell. Pain and suffering for all eternity."

"You should come to church with me, Lach," suggested Jake. "It's not too late for you to be saved."

The conversation drifted to our plans for the summer. We were speculating about the upcoming football season when Mr. Van Dyk arrived with a farmer and tractor. A half-hour later, I was home.

The next day I was sitting under the elm tree in our backyard seeking respite from the heat. We'd been back in Tools Rock almost a year now. Duncan was in high school, I was in middle school and Maggie attended elementary school.

By now, I was resigned to Tools Rock. At first I hated it. No movies. No soldiers. No river. No army base. Nothing but cornfields. And all the people looked alike. I missed my New York friends and our adventures.

When I began school, some of my classmates made fun of my New York accent and my pull-over sweaters. I began wearing flannel shirts and tried to change the way I talked. Then I decided I didn't want to be like Iowa people, so I exaggerated my New York speech and wore my sweaters every day. After I won a fight with Dave Danvers, no one made fun of me anymore. I eventually outgrew my sweaters and my New York speech slowly disappeared.

I was thinking about religion. I didn't realize I was a sinner and I certainly didn't want to burn in Hell throughout eternity. It didn't seem fair. I'd never done anything really bad. If I was a sinner, then all my family must be sinners too. They never went to church and I never heard about anyone being baptized, whatever that was. I didn't like the thought of my family burning in Hell. Mom came from the garden with a basket of peas and sat in the lawn chair beside me.

"I've never known such a long hot spell," she said, shelling the peas. "Reminds me of the summer of '36." I absently took a handful of pods and began shelling them.

"Do you believe in Jesus?" I asked.

Mom was somewhat taken aback. "I don't know. I've never really thought much about it."

"Why don't we go to church?"

"It's never been important to us. Why do you ask?"

"Last night some of the kids were talking. They said all people are sinners until they're baptized and accept Jesus Christ. They said you burn in Hell if you don't."

"Different people believe different things, Lach." She continued shelling peas.

"They said it's in the Bible."

"Lots of things are in the Bible. Some of them are more important to some people than to others. I wouldn't worry about it. The important thing is be a good person and lead a good life."

"They said you gotta go to church and be saved."

"Do you want to go to church, Lach?"

I was quiet for a minute. I picked up another handful of pods and said, "Maybe. I'm not sure."

❧   ❧   ❧

I mowed the yard the next day. After I finished, I decided to visit my friend Ross Hamilton. I wheeled my bike from the garage and pedaled to his house. I knocked on the door and Ross appeared.

"Hi Lach. C'mon in. I was thinking of calling you. Mom went to Carston and I'm alone."

We went to the living room and sat on the sofa.

"What've you been doing?" I asked.

"Not much. I had to pull weeds in the garden, but I quit after Mom left." We were quiet for several moments. "Do you want to look at the pictures?"

"Yeah."

"I'll get them and we'll go up to my room."

Ross went into his parents' bedroom and returned with an envelope. I followed him upstairs and we lay on his bed. He took the pictures from the envelope and gave some to me. We studied them closely.

"Boy, he's really got a big peter! Do you think ours will get that big?"

"Maybe," said Ross, examining a photo of a copulating couple.

Several months previously, Ross discovered the photos on the top shelf of his parents' bedroom closet. He told me about them and one day when his parents were away, he invited me over to see them. Since then we'd repeated the session several times when Ross' parents were gone.

I studied the photos carefully. The naked women didn't interest me much, but I was excited by the big erections of the men and some of the things the women were doing to them.

"He has a lot of hairs," I said, appraising one of the photos.

"Yeah, I got twenty-three now. I wish mine were black like his. You can see them better."

Too soon, Ross said we should put the pictures away before his mother came home. He returned them to their hiding place and we rode our bikes uptown for a cherry coke.

It was Thursday evening and I decided to walk uptown to check-out the band concert. Every Thursday evening during the summer months, the high school band played in the bandstand in the Square. The stores around the Square stayed open until ten so people could shop and enjoy the concert. Others sat on benches or in their cars parked around the Square. Girls, dressed in their best summer dresses, paraded around the bandstand followed by admiring boys, showing-off and teasing them.

I decided to treat myself to a chocolate malt at Wilson's Drug Store. When I entered, Jake de Mier was sitting at the soda fountain with a root beer float. I sat on the stool beside him.

"Hi Lach," said Jake, sucking his straw. "What're you going to have?"

"Chocolate malt." I placed a quarter on the counter. The clerk came and took my order.

"Really hot, eh?" said Jake.

"Yeah."

"Have you been to church yet?"

"No."

BEFORE SUMMER

"Why don't you come with me on Sunday? I told Mom about you and she said I should bring you to church. She said Reverend Vander Weel can probably help you."

I didn't like the idea of Jake spreading the word that I wasn't saved. And I wasn't sure I wanted any help from Reverend Vander Weel, but I was curious to know more about church. It probably wouldn't hurt to be saved. If I was a sinner, I'd have that taken care of.

"I don't know," I said, tackling the big malt the clerk placed before me. The glass was full and more was in the can. That's one of the things I liked about malts. "What time does church begin?"

"Church doesn't start until eleven, but I only go to Sunday school. It starts at ten. Why don't you come? We'll have lots of fun. We really raise hell with old lady Beekstra."

"I don't know," I said again.

"C'mon. You'll like it. I'll stop by your house at quarter to ten and we can walk together. I'll tell you what to do." He sucked noisily through his straw as he finished his root beer float.

"Maybe I will."

"Good. Finish your malt and we'll go see what the stupid girls are doing."

The following Sunday at breakfast, I announced I was attending church with Jake de Mier.

"Is something special happening?" asked Mom.

"No. Jake asked me to go with him, so I thought I'd go."

Dad looked up from his newspaper and muttered, "Damn Dutchmen. They sow their wild oats on Saturday night and then go to church on Sunday morning and pray for crop failure." He returned to his paper.

Duncan snickered, "Lach will probably marry one of those Dutch girls and go to church every Sunday with his Dutch kids."

"Don't be stupid, Dunc."

"Be quiet, Duncan," said Mom. "If Lach wants to go to church that's his business."

Jake arrived and we walked to the Baptist church. When we entered, I recognized most of the people. Everyone was very friendly and told me how happy they were to see me. Reverend Vander Weel stood before the congregation and said a few words of welcome and a prayer. Then, to my embarrassment, he told the congregation that I was visiting and he hoped they would see me at church every Sunday. Everyone turned and smiled at me. I blushed. Then they all sang a dull, monotonous song, following which Reverend Vander Weel said another prayer and dismissed the congregation for Sunday school.

"We go down to the basement," Jake said. I followed him to a small room downstairs where I found some of my least favorite classmates. Nellie Dyksma, who always had bad breath, smiled at me and said, "I'm glad you're going to be saved, Lach."

Mrs. Idabelle Beekstra entered and ordered us to sit down and be quiet. We found chairs, but we weren't quiet. She began the lesson, a continuation of an earlier one about Jesus walking on water. I was amazed.

"How could Jesus walk on water?" I asked.

"Because he was the son of God," smiled Mrs. Beekstra.

"But how did he do it? I mean, what did he have that allowed him to do it?"

"He was the son of God," repeated Mrs. Beekstra firmly. "God let him do it."

Nellie snickered at my ignorance.

"We don't question how God works his wonders," said Mrs. Beekstra. I got the message: Sunday school wasn't a place where you asked questions.

The lesson continued about Jesus curing people and performing miracles. It sounded like fairy tales to me and I never liked fairy tales because they were so preposterous.

When Mrs. Beekstra dismissed Sunday school, she called me aside and said, "I'm so glad to see you here, Lachlan. I always hoped that some of your family would join the church. Perhaps you'll show them the way. God sometimes works through children. Will I see you next week?"

"I don't know. Maybe."

"I hope so," she smiled, sweetly. "God bless you."

Jake came over and announced, "Mom says I have to go to church. C'mon up with me. It'll help you get saved faster."

I hadn't planned on attending the church service, but I was a little curious about what it was all about. I followed Jake upstairs and we found seats beside his parents. They smiled at me. Everyone smiled at me and told me how happy they were to see me. I didn't know why they were so glad to see me. Most of them saw me around town during the week and didn't seem all that happy to see me.

Reverend Vander Weel began the service with a short prayer about God and Jesus and heaven. These seemed

GOD, CHURCH AND JESUS

favorite topics. Then he instructed the congregation to open their hymnals and we all sang a slow, boring song. The Andrews Sisters could certainly teach them how to liven up a song. I was getting restless. The seats were hard and the room was stifling hot.

Reverend Vander Weel announced that a new soul had found their church today. He smiled at me. Everyone turned and smiled at me. I was mortified. Then he told the congregation how fortunate they were to be saved, how God and Jesus loved them, and how they would all live forever in heaven with their loved ones. But, he said, they must help others who hadn't been saved. God sent his son Jesus to die for the sins of the world. He talked about Jesus dying on the cross and his resurrection. He said the world must confess its sins, wash them away and live happily forever with Christ as their Lord.

I couldn't understand why anyone would send his kid someplace where he knew he would get killed. He must have wanted to get rid of him. And how did Jesus get out of that cave where they put him after he died? It sounded like a ghost story and I didn't believe in ghosts. The sermon was long and repetitious. My mind began wandering. I looked around. Several people were dozing, including old Frank Fraken who periodically snorted himself awake. Mrs. Icephena Hefflefinger was savagely laced into her corset and her face grew redder and redder as the service progressed. The Van Zee twins kicked one another in the pew in front of me while Eveline Roosma fanned herself furiously, spreading smells suggesting she missed her Saturday-night bath. Finally, the minister asked us to join him in a prayer that everyone seemed to know. We sang another song, the minister prayed again and the service ended.

Outside on the front steps, Mrs. Beekstra invited me to Vacation Bible School that began the following Monday. I said I would think about it and walked home.

I hadn't enjoyed church very much, but maybe you weren't supposed to enjoy church. Nonetheless, I was still concerned about burning in Hell if I wasn't saved. I burnt my finger once and it hurt several days. I decided to give Bible school a try. I didn't have much to do that week anyway.

When I told my parents I was going to attend the week-long Baptist Bible school, they didn't say anything, but Duncan snickered, "Lach's really getting religious. Soon he'll be sleeping with his Bible."

"Shut up, Dunc."

"If Lach wants to go to Bible school, that's his business," said Mom.

"Boring," said Duncan. He made a face and rolled his eyes.

I attended Bible school the entire week. Once I began, I decided I'd go everyday so I wouldn't miss anything. The classes, a review of the major stories of the Bible, were taught by an elderly woman who couldn't maintain discipline.

Most of the Bible was confusing to me. Like Adam and Eve. I had no idea what their sin was or what was so wrong about eating the apple. When I asked the teacher to explain it, she blushed and told me to read the story again. Adam and Eve's kids must have married one another and had kids of their own, I decided. I asked if it was okay to do that back in those days. The teacher blushed again and said things were done differently then. I learned about Noah who built a boat big enough to carry two of every animal on earth. I couldn't imagine a boat that big. You'd need room for all the food to feed them, too. And some of them would probably fight. And what about plants? Did Noah take plants too? I didn't understand the birth of Jesus at all. How could a woman who didn't do it have a baby? Everyone knew a man and a woman had to do it to make a baby. Joseph must have done it with Mary and they blamed it on God. I stopped asking questions. The teacher usually answered it was God's will or was embarrassed because she didn't know the answer. Maybe the Bible stories were good stories to tell little kids. But grown-up people?

The teacher talked a lot about sin and sinners and how Satan was always trying to tempt people. I suspected that looking at Ross' pictures might be a sin. She talked about Hell and how awful it is. God sends the sinners to Hell and lets Satan hurt them in horrible, painful ways. I didn't get that one either. If God was so powerful, why didn't he make people stop sinning, get rid of Satan and close down Hell?

Each afternoon at the end of class, we were instructed to bow our heads and pray silently. I bowed my head but I didn't pray. I wasn't sure how to do it. More importantly, I wasn't convinced about God and Jesus and all the rest.

The Sunday following Bible school was another scorching, sunny day. The heat wave was entering its third week. I decided it was too hot to go to church. Besides I'd had enough religion. After a light lunch, we sat outdoors in lawn chairs under the big elm tree in the back yard. Mom made a pitcher of lemonade. As we sipped its cool tartness, the sky began darkening.

"Looks like we may be in for a storm," said Dad, standing up and scanning the sky. Jagged streaks of snake-lightning cut through the dark clouds in the east.

"Maybe it'll break this terrible heat," said Mom.

A slight breeze came up, initially warm and then cool. Sprinkles of rain began falling.

"Rain," cried Maggie. She jumped from her chair and ran from under the tree to feel the rain. It began falling faster.

"The windows," said Mom. "Everyone inside to close the windows."

We rushed into the house as the wind grew stronger and the rain fell faster. Suddenly the wind began blowing furiously and leaves and small branches flew past the windows.

"It feels like a tornado," said Dad. The wind rattled the house.

"We'd better go to the basement," said Mom, nervously.

Dad peered out the window and after some hesitation agreed with Mom. I knew it must be bad because Dad never liked to go to the basement during a storm. In the basement, we sat against the north wall and listened to the muffled sounds of the storm raging outside. Eventually the winds subsided and we returned upstairs and checked the destruction. Other than scattered leaves and small limbs, we saw no damage.

"You'd better call the farm and see if they're alright," suggested Dad.

Mom cranked the wall phone and after several tries made it through to Jenny, the operator. She asked about the storm and we waited expectantly as she listened.

"Thanks, Jenny. Could you put me through to the farm?" Mom turned to us. "Most of the damage was south of town, according to Jenny." Then she said to the telephone, "Hello, this is Eliza. Is everything alright out there?"

After learning the farm was unharmed, Duncan and I decided to walk uptown and check-out the damage. We skirted several fallen limbs, but didn't see any damage to houses. When we reached the Square, it was a different story. We joined a cluster of men in front of the remains of the Baptist church. The roof and the front were gone and two sidewalls were collapsed. The church was completely destroyed.

"Strange the way tornadoes work," said Gordon Fraser, our postmaster. "This was the only building it touched on the Square. Then it dropped down two blocks away and took the front porch off Reverend Vander Weel's house."

"Did some pretty serious damage to the Dutch farms south of town," said Keith Marshall of the lumberyard. "My missus called her relatives out there and they said there's quite a bit of damage to buildings and a lot of the corn is flattened."

I looked at the ruined church and listened to the talk of the men. I eventually lost interest and wandered over to the big red rock, walked around it reading the familiar names carved on its surface. I meandered down the street toward home, kicking small branches off the sidewalk and thinking about the storm, the destroyed church and Bible school. All the Baptists were baptized and saved. They attended church every Sunday. But still God let the tornado blow their church away and flatten their corn. Something was wrong with this picture.

"So much for being saved."

I kicked a tin can from the sidewalk and ran the rest of the way home.

Old Fred and Bucky

ONE OF MY Mom's favorite sayings was "Everybody's strange but me and thee, and sometimes I wonder about thee." She always said it when someone did something unusual or different. It was an observation, not a put-down.

Tools Rock had its share of strange people. Some were downright weird, like old Adam Rankin who chewed on the same cigar for days and peed in a bucket in his hardware store and tossed the pee out the front door every Tuesday morning at ten o'clock. Once he drenched Alma Stoper when she was passing by. She had some well-chosen words for the old man that no one realized she knew. Ancient Emily Evans collected bottles and her house was packed with every kind of bottle imaginable. She was tall and skinny and lived in her kitchen because all her other rooms were crammed with bottles. We never trick-or-treated at her house on Halloween because we thought she was a witch. She had a big wart on her nose. Then there were the Strucker brothers, the grave-diggers for Tools Rock who spent their idle summer hours lounging among the tombstones at Silent Hill Cemetery.

Old Fred Mathers was a strange one too, but not in a weird way. Everyone liked Old Fred. We always called him "Old Fred," not just "Fred." I'm not sure how old he was, but he seemed ancient to us kids. With white hair, crackling blue eyes and a crooked smile, he was a little man, no taller than some of the tall boys. If he was ever married, no one knew about it. He always wore bib overalls, a denim shirt and clodhopper shoes. His clothes were clean and his kitchen neat, unlike old Ben Barnes who lived in a filthy one-room shack near the railroad tracks, never shaved, never changed clothes and took a bath about once a year—if that often. Old Fred was one of those old people everyone saw everyday but no one really knew much about. They had outlived their peers and what family remained was distant or much younger and not interested in claiming them. There weren't too many old people like that in Tools Rock, but there were a few.

Old Fred lived not too far from us in a ramshackle house at the edge of town with a big pasture where he kept his old horse Bucky and his cow Sally. He had an outdoor toilet and pumped his water from a well outside his kitchen door. Each summer, he carefully tended a circular bed of lavender petunias in his front yard. He once told me they were his mother's favorite flower. He kept a few chickens and sold eggs when he had extra ones. Mom always said Old Fred went to bed with the chickens, and for a long time I thought she meant that he slept with his chickens—rather than going to sleep at sunset as they did. Bucky's barn was a patchwork-quilt sort of shack built by Old Fred with scraps of lumber. A door connected the house and barn and for all intents and purposes the old man and

OLD FRED AND BUCKY

Bucky lived together. Some people said Old Fred slept on a straw bed in the barn with Bucky during the summertime, but I'm not sure that was true. Once I asked him how old Bucky was. He said he didn't know, but he'd been around for donkey ears. Sally the cow was younger and had her own little barn where she was milked and spent the nights.

Bucky was a big brown work-horse, which is what we called those gigantic farm animals once central to Iowa farms. Most farmers had tractors but a few still kept horses left over from the pre-tractor days to handle the jobs tractors couldn't do. The horses always had names. Daisy, Big Red, Patsy and Old Bob were some of the ones I remember. Most were "out to pasture," meaning they were retired from farm work. Farmers frequently became attached to their horses and let them live out their final days on the farm. A few sent them to the rendering works where they were euthanized and their remains made into all sorts of things I never wanted to contemplate, the most harmless being the glue made from their hooves.

Old Fred was the town's handyman. If you needed something done that didn't require special skills, he was the man you called. He would dig a new hole for your outdoor toilet, spade your flower beds, mow your yard, rake your leaves or shovel the snow from your sidewalks. He and Bucky would haul your trash to the dump or deliver your coal from the coal yard in their rickety old wagon. But spring was their busiest season when they plowed the gardens of Tools Rock. Most houses had big gardens, the produce of which fed the families during the summer months and the surplus was canned for winter consumption. After the ground thawed and the spring rains let-up,

Old Fred and Bucky made their rounds. They had a homemade two-wheeled rig for the plow which Bucky pulled to the gardens. Old Fred would unload the plow, hook it to Bucky and turn up the rich black soil. Then they moved on to the next garden and before long, all the gardens of Tools Rock were ready for planting. Old Fred would even plant your garden if you wanted him to, but most people, like my Dad, preferred to plant their own. No one had to call Old Fred, not that he had a telephone. He decided when it was time to plow and showed up with Bucky. He never requested payment, but everyone paid him prices they'd worked out over the years. If you weren't home when he finished plowing, you went to his house and paid him. He never came to collect and always seemed embarrassed to take your money, saying it really wasn't necessary to pay him. But everyone knew the old man's livelihood depended on the money, so no one ever tried to cheat him.

Old Fred maintained a sizeable patch of land along the railroad tracks at the edge of town. It wasn't clear if he had permission to use the land, but he farmed it year after year with no apparent complaints from the railroad. He'd plow it in the spring and plant it in potatoes, corn, tomatoes and green beans which he tenderly nursed to maturity. Then, with Bucky beside him, he sat under a makeshift sunscreen in the mornings and late afternoons selling his produce to the Tools Rock housewives for their dinners, suppers and cellars.

OLD FRED AND BUCKY

We kids liked to hang out with Old Fred. He let us ride Bucky around his pasture. He always told us to be good to Bucky. Maybe Bucky couldn't talk but he understood and had feelings, so we were careful what we said around Bucky. During Old Fred's runs to the dump south of town, we sometimes rode with him in the wagon and helped him unload the trash. In the spring and summer, we played softball in his pasture even though it meant a slightly uphill grade to our game. That same grade provided sledding for us in the snowy winter months.

One of my favorite places was Indian Creek, the little stream that ran along the bottom of Old Fred's pasture. During hot summer days, I liked to go down there for a cool drink of water from the springs that seeped through its banks. Ross and I always visited the creek in early spring checking out the tadpoles. We'd take some home in jars and each year were amazed when they sprouted legs and turned into frogs. Mom always insisted we return the little frogs to the creek where they could live out their lives in their natural habitat.

Old Fred was the bee-man of Tools Rock. He had about a half-dozen bee hives in his pasture. If bees swarmed somewhere in town, Old Fred was the one you called to take care of them. One day bees swarmed in our backyard. A cloud of them flew over the garden and congregated in a huge mass in our peach tree weighing its limbs near to breaking. Dad sent me over to Old Fred's to ask if he would come and get the bees.

I knocked on his front door, but received no response. "Old Fred, Old Fred," I called. I ran behind the house and saw him in the pasture examining one of Bucky's hooves.

"What's the matter, Boy?" he asked. He always called us boys "Boy."

"We got a bunch of bees in the peach tree. Dad wants you to get them."

Old Fred didn't say anything. I followed him to the barn where he fired up his smoker, put on his hat and veil, and returned home with me carrying an empty hive. He looked like a scary Halloween disguise. He walked around the peach tree, appraising the mass of humming bees in its branches. He placed the hive nearby and with the aid of his smoker, directed the bees toward the empty hive. Soon they were ensconced in their new home.

"I'll come back and get them this evening when they're all tucked away for the night," he said.

"Okay," said Dad. "Thanks for coming over."

"My thanks to you. Always happy to add some new critters to my hives. Much obliged, much obliged." He collected his gear and headed home.

Old Fred sold some of his honey, but much of it he gave away—mostly to us kids. Whenever we had a sweet tooth, we'd go to Old Fred's place and hang around until he offered us some honey. He'd pull a slab of comb from his storage room, cut-off pieces, and we'd chomp into the sweet gooey mess, sucking the honey from the comb and then chewing the wax until we tired of it. He always asked us to return the wax. I'm not sure what he did with it, but Mom said people once used it for making candles.

OLD FRED AND BUCKY

Old Fred had electricity in his house so I don't think he used it for candles.

My Dad loved his garden. We ate fresh produce from it during the summer and Mom canned the surplus for winter consumption. Dad did most of the gardening, but occasionally he made me and Maggie help him out. Our least favorite job was crawling up and down the garden rows picking tomato worms and potato bugs from the infested plants and dropping them into water buckets. Dad was a purist about his garden and never used pesticides. Besides there weren't many around in those days and Dad probably didn't want to shell out money for them. When Maggie and I finished, I carried the buckets of pests to Old Fred's place.

"Much obliged, much obliged, Boy," he said, taking the buckets. "The girls will like 'em. Much obliged." He then scattered the bugs and worms over his yard and his chickens came running for a feeding frenzy. The next time I visited him, he always gave me some eggs to take home.

We bought our milk from Old Fred and his cow Sally. Every other evening, I'd walk to Old Fred's place with a half-gallon glass canning jar. I'd knock on his kitchen door and he'd call, "Come on in, Boy." I'd enter his kitchen, hand him the jar and he'd carefully fill it from the milk bucket he kept covered with a towel in a corner. I'd give him a quarter, take the jar and return home. Once I dropped the jar on my way home, breaking it and spilling the milk. I didn't know whether to go home or back to

Old Fred's place. I decided to go back. Old Fred answered my knock.

"I dropped the milk, Old Fred," I said sheepishly.

He simply said, "That's okay, Boy. Accidents happen." He went to his backroom and returned with a half-gallon glass jar and filled it with Sally's milk.

"I don't have another quarter."

He smiled his crooked smile and said, "Don't worry, Boy. Accidents happen."

Sally died unexpectedly. One afternoon, Old Fred went into the pasture and she was dead. Word soon spread among us kids that Sally died and Ross and I ghoulishly hurried over to Old Fred's to see her body. We pestered him with questions, but all Old Fred would say is, "It was her time. That's the way it is. Everything has its time, and it was Sally's time." He was digging a hole beside her body.

"Are you going to bury her?"

"Yep. Right here where she can be with us."

"Do you have any more shovels? We'll help you."

"Look in the shed over there, Boy."

We ran to the shed and came back with two shovels and started digging beside Old Fred. It was hard work and we kept asking Old Fred if it was deep enough yet, but he said no, it had to be deeper. Finally, he was satisfied with the depth. He tied ropes around Sally and we pulled and tugged with the other kids who had gathered until her carcass fell into the hole.

"Let's look at her awhile before we cover her," said Old Fred. "It was her time."

OLD FRED AND BUCKY

We stood quietly gazing into the open grave with Bucky looking over our shoulders. I picked some blossoms from a nearby Black-Eyed Susan bush and dropped them into the grave.

"That's nice," said Old Fred. "She'll like 'em." He was quiet for several more minutes and then said, "Okay. Let's cover her up."

Old Fred didn't get another cow and we had to buy our milk at the store. It took us awhile to get used to the taste. Sally's grave became our pitching mound when we played ball in the pasture the following spring.

Old Fred had a maze of outbuildings in his backyard that hooked-up to the back of his house. He was always building another shack with some scrap lumber someone gave him or he salvaged from a construction site or an abandoned house. Ross and I explored the labyrinth of shacks with Old Fred on those days when we trailed after him with nothing else to do. Occasionally, we slipped into a shack on our own for a smoke. Once Old Fred said, "I don't want you boys smoking back there."

We were surprised and embarrassed. Ross looked at me guiltily. We didn't realize he knew we visited his shacks. "We're not smoking very much," said Ross.

"Okay then. We don't want any fires. Be careful." He smiled. "You boys will be boys."

I remember when Bucky died. It was a few days after summer vacation began and I was having trouble finding something to do. I decided to visit Old Fred. Something was usually happening at his place.

BEFORE SUMMER

His kitchen door was closed when I arrived which was strange because it was usually open during the summer. I knocked on it and waited. No response. I knocked again. Still no response. I yelled, "Old Fred! Are you there?"

A small voice from inside said, "I'm here, Boy. Come on in."

I turned the knob and the door opened. Old Fred was lying on the daybed he kept in his kitchen.

"Are you okay, Old Fred?"

"I'm okay. Just a little tuckered today. A little tuckered." He was quiet and then said, "Bucky died last night." He was staring straight ahead at the old 1938 calendar that he kept on his wall because he liked its picture of baby chickens.

"Oh no!" I cried. I was genuinely saddened. Bucky was one of the constants in my life. "What happened?"

"I guess it was his time," said Old Fred, still lying on the daybed. "We all have our time, and it was Bucky's time."

"Where is he?"

"In the pasture." He added, "I reckon I should get up and bury him."

"I'll help you," I volunteered. "I'll get Ross and some other kids, and we'll help."

"I'd be much obliged. For some reason, I'm really tuckered-out today."

"I'll be right back." I ran home and told Mom about Bucky. Then I jumped on my bike and headed toward Ross' house, spreading the news about Bucky along the way. When I passed the telephone office, Jenny Mason was sitting in the window, taking a break from the switchboard.

"Bucky died," I shouted.

"Oh no," she said. "That's terrible. What happened?"

"Don't know. Old Fred found him dead. Ross and I are going to help bury him."

Jenny left the window. I knew she was headed for the switchboard to spread the news about Bucky.

Ross was shocked when I told him about Bucky and returned to Old Fred's house with me. He was still lying on the daybed in the kitchen.

"We'll dig a grave for Bucky," I said. "Where should we dig it?"

"Right beside him. We can't move him. He's too big. He'll be near Sally. I'll come out in a few minutes. I need a little more time. I guess it was Bucky's time."

Ross and I went outdoors, found some shovels in an old shed and began digging a hole beside Bucky. News of the horse's death spread throughout town, and before long, people began arriving in the pasture. Mr. Fraser, the postmaster, and Hank Hanson, who owned the Southside Tavern, brought shovels and relieved me and Ross.

"Where's Old Fred?" Mom asked me when she arrived.

"He's inside. He said he needed more time."

Mom said nothing, but walked to the house and entered Old Fred's kitchen door. We continued digging as more people arrived. Even our old neighbor Miss Cotters showed up. I was surprised. She almost never left her house for anything. Most people quietly watched us dig, others walked over to the dead horse, looking at him sadly.

"I think it's deep enough," said Dad. He and several men secured ropes to Bucky and they were joined by others and pulled the dead horse into the grave.

"We better get Old Fred now," said Mr. Fraser. "Go get him, Lach."

I ran to Old Fred's house and entered the back door. He and Mom were sitting at the kitchen table. She was holding Old Fred's hand. His eyes were glistening. "Dad says it's time to bury Bucky," I said.

Old Fred was quiet for several moments and then said, "Okay Boy. I'm ready now." He slowly rose from his chair and we left the house and joined the people in the pasture. Old Fred registered no surprise at the crowd, but murmured "Much obliged. Much obliged I'm sure. Much obliged to you all," as he passed among them to the hole where Bucky lay. He stood looking down at Bucky. Mom stood beside him. Idabelle Beekstra stepped forward with a bouquet of zinnias and quietly dropped them into the grave.

"Much obliged," murmured Old Fred. "Much obliged. I'm sure Bucky's much obliged too."

Everyone stood solemnly around the grave. A rooster's crow broke the silence.

"It was Bucky's time," said Old Fred quietly, a single tear running down his cheek. "Everyone and everything has its time. This was Bucky's time." Then after several moments of silence, he said. "We'd better cover him now."

The men began tossing shovelfuls of dirt into the grave. Old Fred said to no one in particular, "I'm plumb tuckered-out today. I better go back inside. Much obliged to you all, I'm sure. Much obliged, much obliged. It was Bucky's time." He slowly walked toward his house with Mom at his side.

OLD FRED AND BUCKY

I lucked out. I had a great mom. A good mom takes you a long way in life. My mom's universe was pretty much her family, her domestic one and her extended one. Occasionally, however, her interests extended beyond that circle. And that's what happened after Bucky died. Probably more than anyone else, she sensed how saddened Old Fred was by Bucky's death. She visited the old man often with gifts of food, and she sent me over on days when she couldn't go. About two weeks after Bucky's death, she decided it would be a good gesture if some of the townspeople bought Old Fred a horse. We were sitting at the table one evening after supper when she proposed to Dad the idea of taking a collection to buy a horse.

"I don't know, Eliza," he said. "Old Fred might think it's charity and you know how independent he is."

"But it would be a gift. Everyone misses Bucky. It's for the town, not just Old Fred."

"Maybe it would be better if you found a horse someone doesn't want anymore. Old Fred could adopt it."

"I suppose the first thing I should do is see if Old Fred is interested in having another horse." She stood and began clearing the table as the rest of us dispersed. It was Maggie's turn to help wash dishes so I went into the living room and listened to Fibber Magee and Molly on the radio.

I was with Mom when she talked to Old Fred about a new horse. She had canned some sweet pickles that morning and decided to take a jar to him. He met us at the kitchen door and invited us in. We sat at the kitchen table with its faded blue oilcloth. I noticed for the first time that the old worn linoleum on the floor was the same shade of blue. I also noticed that each of his four kitchen chairs was different from the others. A twisted ribbon of sticky fly paper covered with dead flies hung from the ceiling.

"Much obliged for the pickles, Mrs. MacLennan," said Old Fred. "I'm sure I'll enjoy them." He held the jar to the light. "Looks like the kind my poor old mother used to make."

After more small talk, Mom said, "Have you ever thought about getting another horse, Old Fred?"

He didn't answer immediately, but after several moments, he said, "I think my horse days are gone, Mrs. MacLennan. Couldn't break-in another one. Bucky and I understood each other. Wouldn't be right to get another horse. I'm gettin' old. I'm not gonna be around too much longer."

"You'll probably outlive us all, Old Fred." Mom smiled and patted his hand.

Old Fred didn't outlive us all, but he did live several more years. I grew older with other interests and saw him less. When spring came, we missed him and Bucky plowing our gardens, but by then people were buying garden tractors and plowing their own gardens. Mom continued to visit Old Fred with gifts of food, but most people didn't see him anymore. He seldom left his house which became even more ramshackle.

One October morning, Mom and I took some soup to Old Fred. He'd been feeling under the weather and didn't have a lot to say during our visit. But as we were leaving, he said, "Mrs. MacLennan, you've always been good to me. I want you to know that I 'preciate it. I'm mighty obliged, mighty obliged. You're a good woman, Mrs. MacLennan. You'll have stars in your crown." He looked at me and said, "You're a lucky boy to have such a good mother."

I didn't know what to say, so I said nothing.

Mom smiled at him and said, "Thank you, Old Fred. It's easy to be good to you. You're a good man."

The next day Mom went back to check on him. When she knocked on the kitchen door, there was no response. She went inside and called his name as she explored the other rooms. Not finding him, she went into the old barn attached to the kitchen. She found him.

Old Fred lay dead on his straw bed in Bucky's stall.

It was his time.

Miss Cotters

"AND HERE'S A nice piece of banana cake for you, Lachlan. I baked it this morning."

I wondered how many times I'd heard Miss Cotters say that. Since I began doing chores for her as a little kid before the war, Miss Cotters always gave me a piece of banana cake when I finished. It was good cake and I still liked it as much as I did when I was little.

"Are you looking forward to school, Lachlan?" she asked, interrupting my thoughts.

"Yes I am, Miss Cotters. I'll be in eighth grade this year." I swallowed my last bite of cake and placed the fork on the plate. She always gave me the same plate and the same fork. I knew because the blue plate had a small chip and one of the points of the fork was slightly bent.

I looked around the familiar kitchen. Miss Cotters was washing dishes in a dishpan on the cabinet counter. Everything in the room was old and worn, but sparkling clean. It probably was worn because Miss Cotters cleaned it so often. She didn't have much else to do.

Miss Cotters lived in a white Victorian house across the garden from us with her invalid brother Edward who seldom left his bed. I never knew what was wrong with him, but he'd been ailing ever since I could remember. Each time I came to do chores, I had to say hello to Edward. I dreaded it, but I knew the old man enjoyed seeing me, so I always went into his bedroom and gave the same answers to the same questions.

"How are you today, Lachlan?"

"I'm fine, sir."

"You're growing into such a big strong young man," he said, looking me over appraisingly. "And how is school?"

He always asked that, even if school wasn't in session, and I always said, "School is fine, sir."

"And your mother and father?"

"They're fine, sir."

"It's always good to see you, Lachlan. You be a good boy now."

"Yes, sir."

Then Miss Cotters would take me to the kitchen and give me my piece of cake and whatever money she owed me. I mowed her yard and helped her pull weeds in the summer. I raked her leaves in the fall and in the winter, I shoveled her sidewalks, carried in her coal and hauled out her ashes. In the spring, I helped prepare her garden and flowerbeds.

The Cotterses had always kept to themselves. The father died many years before I was born and the sickly mother insisted the children remain home and care for her. Edward became ill also and it was Miss Cotters' duty to care for them both. The mother occasionally became deranged, escaped the house and wandered uptown in her bathrobe, stopping people on the street and glaring at them with burning eyes, her long white hair askew. Someone always brought her home and Miss Cotters was embarrassed and apologetic. Early one cold January morning, the old woman ended her life on the back porch by submerging her head in a bucket of water. I never understood how she could drown herself that way. She must've really wanted to die.

Miss Cotters was a skinny woman who looked older than her fifty-some years. Her dark hair was worn in a tight bun and her pale blue eyes always seemed slightly startled behind her wire-framed glasses. Each Saturday morning at ten o'clock, she drove her black Model-A Ford uptown to buy groceries. Her purchases varied somewhat with her needs, but she always bought a canned diet drink. She wore black clothes, complete with hat, veil and gloves on her Saturday shopping excursions. Heavy white powder gave her a ghostly specter. Duncan said she looked like a corpse at a funeral. When she returned home, she unloaded the groceries, drove the Model-A into the garage and locked it securely. She hadn't left the property for any other reason since her mother's funeral. And that was the only time anyone had seen Edward leave the house since he became bedridden many years previously. He attended the funeral in a wheelchair and the ordeal was almost too much for him.

Most people in Tools Rock were related to one another, but no one claimed relationship to the Cotterses. No one knew where they came from. Miss Cotters was very frugal, but she never complained about not having enough money. Only two rooms of the old Victorian house were heated in the winter, the kitchen and Edward's bedroom. At night, a forty-watt light bulb illuminated Edward's room until eight o'clock when they punctually retired.

I walked home across the garden and found Mom ironing clothes. I went to my room and lay on my bed, thinking of some way to spend the rest of the day. I thought of Ross Hamilton and the pictures. Then I remembered he was still away on vacation.

The following week, I mowed Miss Cotters' lawn. When I finished she invited me into the house. After my usual conversation with Edward, she called me to the kitchen where my banana cake waited.

"You like school, don't you, Lachlan," she said, watching me eat.

"Most of the time."

"I'm sure you're a good student."

"Thank you, Miss Cotters. I guess I am."

"I liked school so much," she said after a short pause. "Latin was my favorite subject. Have you studied Latin, Lachlan?"

"No, ma'am. It's not offered."

"That's too bad. You learn so much from Latin. I loved to read about the Romans. What a glorious time that was. I still have my books and on Wednesday and Friday afternoons, I spend two hours studying my Latin."

I could think of nothing to say so I remained silent.

"Sometimes I wish I were young again. Those were the happiest days of my life, when I was a student. I was a very good student."

"I bet you were."

She smiled at me. "Latin and history were my favorite subjects. I always found the past appealing."

"Why was that?"

She thought a moment. "I'm not sure. Maybe because you know what it was like, and you can choose the parts you want to read about. You're not surprised and you don't have to read about the bad things unless you want to." She paused again and watched a robin feed its fledglings in the tree outside the window. "The present has always been unappealing to me. And the future will probably be more of the present. But with the past you can sort it out into only the good things. Sometimes you have to do that." Her voice trailed off. "But sometimes there aren't too many good things."

"I like history too."

"I'm sure you do. And I'm sure you're very good at it."

"I have some *National Geographic* magazines. I'll bring them over and you can look at them."

"Oh joy!" said Miss Cotters, alarmed. "Oh joy!" was her strongest expletive. "I never look at magazines or newspapers. I don't even listen to the radio anymore. They remind me of things I never had and never will have. They make me sad."

An awkward pause made me uncomfortable. I said, "I better go now."

Miss Cotters smiled at me. "And here's your money, Lachlan. Thank you so much. You always do such a good job. I don't know what I'd do without you."

❖ ❖ ❖

MISS COTTERS

I was in the living room playing my Andrews Sisters records. They reminded me of my good times in New York. Ross called earlier and told me the Sun Players were coming next week. The traveling tent show came to Tools Rock each summer and presented four evenings of plays. Ross and I and other boys around town helped put up the big tent and got free passes to one of the performances.

"Don't you get tired of listening to those same old records?" asked Mom as she came into the room. She didn't wait for a reply. "I saw Miss Cotters in the garden and she asked if you would go over and open her kitchen window. It's stuck. God only knows when it was last open."

I switched off the Victrola and put the records away. I walked across the garden and knocked on Miss Cotters' backdoor.

She appeared at the door somewhat flustered. "Oh Lachlan, I'm so glad you could come. I've tried and tried to open the window but it won't budge. Then I thought of you. You're such a strong boy, I'm sure you can open it. Come in."

She opened the door and led me to the window. I tried to raise it but it wouldn't budge. I thumped the frame a couple of times and tried again. It rose about a foot.

"I knew you could open it, Lachlan. Thank you so much. Sit and talk for a minute." She pulled a chair from the table, "I'm sorry I don't have any cake today. I wasn't expecting you."

"That's okay," I said, sitting in the chair. "I'm not hungry anyway."

"You look so much like your Aunt Letha," she said, sitting across from me. "You have the same green eyes and dark hair."

"Did you know my Aunt Letha?"

"I didn't know her well, but of course I saw her around town. This is such a small place. I always thought she was very beautiful."

"So did I."

"I admired her so much. She wanted to improve herself. It was very brave of her to go to Chicago. And she went to college too."

"Dad says she was stubborn."

"I would say 'determined'," said Miss Cotters after a brief pause. "Do you plan to go to college, Lachlan?"

"I don't know. It seems like a long time away. But I know I'm not going to stay here. I'm going to travel all over the world."

"Oh yes, you must travel," said Miss Cotters excitedly. "I wanted to travel too. Don't let them stop you, Lachlan. Not like they did me."

"Who stopped you, Miss Cotters?"

She thought for a moment. "It was mostly Papa. I wanted to go to college so badly. I wanted to become a teacher, a Latin teacher. I begged and begged Mama and Papa. I told them I would repay any money they spent on me. Finally, they decided to let me go. I spent the entire summer after I graduated from high school getting ready. I made three new dresses; one of them was beautiful dark green velvet. I bought the velvet at Shaw's in Carston. I sewed new collars and ribbons on some of my old dresses. I bought notebooks and a new dictionary. I still have them.

MISS COTTERS

I was going to Cedar Falls. I know I would have been a good student—and a good teacher."

"What happened?"

Miss Cotters was quiet a moment and then continued. "It was the morning I was supposed to leave. I was going to ride to Cedar Falls with Gloria Van Meter and her parents. She was entering her sophomore year that fall. When I came down for breakfast—I was so excited I'd hardly slept—Papa met me at the bottom of the stairs and told me I couldn't go. He said he thought about it all night long and decided that going away to college was not proper for a young girl. And besides, he said, they needed me to help out at home. I couldn't believe it."

"What did you do?"

"What could I do? When Papa made up his mind there was no changing it. I pleaded with him. I begged Mama to help me, but she agreed with Papa. Even Edward thought I shouldn't go. When the Van Meters came, Papa told them I was staying home. I went to my room and cried all day. I thought I would die. I've never hurt so much in my life."

She was quiet. I said nothing.

"I suppose it was just as well," she continued, unconvincingly. "Papa had a stroke that winter and Mama could not have cared for him alone. Then after Papa died, Mama became worse and I had to care for her all those years. And now Edward."

"Maybe someday you can leave. You're not so old."

She smiled at me sadly. "No, Lachlan. It's too late. The part of me that wanted to leave is dead now. I don't even hurt anymore." She looked at me and then stiffened angrily. "But don't let it happen to you, Lachlan. Don't let them stop you from leaving. This place does terrible things to you." Her eyes wandered sadly around the kitchen. "Terrible, terrible things."

I didn't know what to say. "I better go home now."

"Thank you so much, Lachlan. I don't know what I'd do without you."

I went home and listened to more of my Andrews Sisters records and remembered what Miss Cotters said about Letha. I decided to go uptown and carve Letha's name on the big red rock in the Square, something I'd planned doing for some time.

A mini-scandal kept Tools Rock gossiping the next few weeks. Greta Parsons, wife of Garth Parsons who operated the butcher shop, ran away with a farm equipment salesman who occasionally visited town. No one was aware she knew the man. One afternoon a strange car parked outside the Parsons' house and a neighbor saw Greta packing the back seat and trunk with boxes. That evening when Garth came home for supper, he couldn't find his wife. He called her sisters and talked to the neighbors, but they knew nothing, except the one who saw her packing the car in the driveway. Later that evening, Western Union called with a telegram for Garth. It was from Greta saying she'd left him and planned to file for divorce. The town was shocked.

Several days after the incident, I was helping Miss Cotters weed her flowerbeds.

"Let's take a rest," she said. "I'll get some cold water." She went into the house and I sat on a bench under the big maple tree that shaded much of the Cotters' backyard. She returned with two glasses of water, handed one to me and sat beside me.

"Wasn't it awful about Greta Parsons?" I said, parroting what everyone in town was saying. "I feel sorry for poor Mr. Parsons."

Miss Cotters was quiet for a moment and then said, "Don't be sad, Lachlan. I'm sure they'll both be happier in the long run. Maybe Mr. Parsons is unhappy now, but he'll probably thank Mrs. Parsons someday."

"Why?" I asked, puzzled.

"Most marriages are awful, Lachlan. Haven't you noticed? After the first few years—sometimes even months—couples begin resenting one another. Sometimes they hate one another."

"Really?" I was genuinely surprised. "Are my Mom and Dad like that?"

"Oh no," said Miss Cotters quickly, looking embarrassed. "Your parents are different." I wasn't sure she really thought so. "When children come along that makes a difference. For a while anyway. They provide a diversion. But when they're gone, the husband and wife are stuck with each other. They spend the rest of their lives looking across the breakfast table wondering who will die first so the other can have some freedom."

"I didn't know that," I said.

"Maybe I'm exaggerating," said Miss Cotters, watching two butterflies visit her flowerbed, "but most people aren't very happy in their relationships, whether it's family or friends. We get stuck with people for a lifetime and we stop growing. We talk about the same old things and see the world the same old way. Greta Parsons has a new life. She has a new man and she's moving to a new place where she'll meet new people. She's lucky and I admire her spunk." She looked at me. "Oh joy! I shouldn't be saying such things to you. You're too young to understand. You probably think I'm a crazy old woman."

"I don't think you're crazy, Miss Cotters." A little strange maybe, but not crazy. "You've always been nice to me."

"Thank you, Lachlan. You're a good boy. Let's finish our weeding."

Ross and I helped put up the tent for the Sun Players. We chose passes to the Saturday night play because it was usually the best one. A local talent show preceded it and after the main play, a special late show was staged for adults only. Last year, Ross and I rehearsed a duet to sing in the talent show, but we got cold feet at the last minute and withdrew. We were too young to see the adult show, but with other boys, we usually peeked under the tent. It was never as risqué as advertised and I couldn't understand what all the fuss was about.

"Thank you for bringing them over," said Miss Cotters. "I've heard the music so often from your house. I'm curious to hear them."

The last time I mowed Miss Cotters' yard she expressed interest in the records I always played. I told her it was the Andrews Sisters. I was amazed that she'd never heard of them and told her I'd bring the Victrola over that afternoon and play some records. She was enthusiastic.

"This is my favorite," I said, placing the needle on the record. "'The Boogie Woogie Bugle Boy.' It's a little scratchy."

Miss Cotters listened to the song and exclaimed, "It certainly is lively." She laughed and clapped her hands.

When the record finished, I played "Rum and Coca-Cola."

"Oh joy! It seems a little naughty."

"Not really," I said, having forgotten the lyrics were rather suggestive. "Here's a funny one." I placed "Mister Five by Five" on the turntable.

Halfway through the record, we heard a voice call "Maude."

"Excuse me. It's Edward." I didn't know her name was Maude. The record finished and I waited for her return before playing another.

A few minutes later, Miss Cotters came into the room looking unhappy. "I'm afraid that will be all the music for today, Lachlan. Edward has a headache and the music is upsetting him. I'm sorry."

"That's okay. Maybe some other time when Edward's feeling better." I unplugged the Victrola and gathered up the records.

"Do you have any church music? Edward might like that."

"I'm sorry Miss Cotters, but I don't have any church music."

Miss Cotters asked me to pull weeds from the hollyhocks that grew along the alley behind her garage. It was a warm, sunny late-August morning and I was enjoying the privacy of the back alley. I liked hollyhocks. Mom once showed me how to make dolls by attaching the upside down blossoms to the buds. Some hollyhocks had gone to seed and I remembered that the seedpods looked like little wheels.

I was looking forward to the beginning of school. I would have a new teacher and maybe there'd be some new students. I was tired of summer. I still sometimes thought about New York and missed the adventures of my days there.

"Lachlan! Lachlan!" Miss Cotters' shouts interrupted my thoughts. I ran from behind the garage and saw her standing at the back door. "Lachlan, please get your mother. Edward's very sick."

I raced across the garden and found Mom in the kitchen making bread. I told her Edward was sick and Miss Cotters wanted her to come. She wiped her hands on a towel, removed her apron and hurried across the garden with me. She knocked on the backdoor and called, "Miss Cotters. It's Eliza MacLennan. Can I help you?"

"Oh yes. Please come in."

Mom and I entered the house and found Miss Cotters in Edward's bedroom. She was agitated and paler than usual.

"I don't know what happened. I heard him call. When I came in, he was like this."

Edward looked terrible. His eyes were glassy, his pallor deathly, and his twisted mouth drooled saliva down his chin as he made guttural sounds.

"I'm afraid he's had a stroke," said Mom. "Get Dr. Horton, Lach. Take your bike. It's probably quicker than trying to get through on the telephone."

"Oh joy! We never go to the doctor."

"Your brother is very sick," said Mom. "He needs a doctor. Hurry Lach."

I rushed home, jumped on my bike and pedaled furiously to Dr. Horton's office some three blocks away. He was in his office and after I told him about Edward, he said he would come immediately and began stuffing medical paraphernalia into his bag. I ran from the office, remounted my bike and returned to the Cotters' house.

Within minutes, Dr. Horton arrived and went directly to Edward without saying a word. I didn't care much for Dr. Horton. He was grossly fat, gruff and always smelled of tobacco and alcohol. But he was the only doctor in town and people said he was the best doctor around when he was sober. He seemed sober this morning.

"He's had a stroke," said Dr. Horton, confirming Mom's diagnosis. "He's pretty bad. We better get him to a hospital."

"Oh joy!" cried Miss Cotters. "Not a hospital!"

"He'll die if he doesn't go to the hospital," said the doctor firmly.

Mom put her arm around Miss Cotters and said, "It's the only thing to do, Miss Cotters."

Miss Cotters cried softly and said, "I don't know, I don't know what to do."

"They'll know how to care for him at the hospital."

"If you think so," Miss Cotters said, hesitantly.

"Where's the telephone?" asked Dr. Horton. "I'll call for an ambulance."

"She doesn't have a phone," said Mom. "Lach, take Dr. Horton home and show him where our phone is."

"No phone," grumbled the doctor. "Everyone has a phone this day and age." He followed me across the garden and into the house where he called the county hospital for an ambulance. When we returned, Miss Cotters was crying hysterically as Mom tried to comfort her.

Edward looked grotesque. His head was thrown back, his eyes and mouth were wide open. I'd seen only one dead person in my life, but I knew Edward was dead. The doctor examined him and pulled the sheet over his face.

"What will I do?" cried Miss Cotters. "What will I do? Edward is all I have. What will I do? What will I do?"

Our entire family went to Edward's funeral, albeit somewhat reluctantly. Mom insisted that because we'd been neighbors to the Cotterses for so many years, it was appropriate we all attend. She was glad we did because the only other attendees were old Hazel Runnels and ancient Gertrude Manners who ghoulishly attended every funeral in Tools Rock. Mom made the funeral arrangements. Miss Cotters was befuddled and said she had no relatives to help her.

School was in its second month. I was playing junior high football, not because I liked it, but I was big and athletic so there seemed no choice but to play. Secretly, I thought it a dumb game.

MISS COTTERS

It was a gray October Saturday morning. Earlier in the week, Miss Cotters had asked me to rake her leaves. It was not a job I liked, but it was mindless and gave me a chance to think about other things and make a little money. Since Edward's death, Miss Cotters seemed sadder and more distant. She still drove to the grocery store each Saturday to buy her diet drink, but no one ever saw a light in her house at night. She rarely left her home and I only saw her when I did her chores and she kept me company while I ate the banana cake she still baked for me. She sat quietly and watched me eat. I tried to engage her in conversation, but she had little to say. I dreaded the visits I used to enjoy. I felt sorry for her but could think of no way to help her. Mom sometimes gave her gifts of food which she quietly accepted. Most of it sat on her kitchen cabinet uneaten. I didn't think she could become skinnier, but she did. She looked like a skeleton.

I finished raking. I scattered the final leaves over the garden and cleaned my rake. I went to Miss Cotters' back porch and knocked on the screen door, but received no response. I knocked again and waited several moments, but still no response. I knocked louder. Miss Cotters always responded to my knocks—in fact, she was usually waiting for me at the door when I finished my chores. I peered through the screen wire and started. Miss Cotters was lying on the porch floor. I tried to open the door, but it was locked. I ran across the garden and found Duncan and Mom in the kitchen.

Mom was calm when I explained what I'd seen. She said, "I'll call the doctor and then we'll go over."

A few minutes later, we met Doctor Horton at the back door of Miss Cotters' house. The doctor told Duncan to break in the screen door, which he easily did. We entered the porch.

Miss Cotters lay on the floor beside an overturned bucket. She was dressed in the black clothes she wore on her Saturday morning shopping excursions. Her head and shoulders were wet and water puddled around her.

"My God," said Dr. Horton. "She drowned herself. Just like her mother."

Mom sighed quietly, tears flooding her eyes, "The poor, poor desperate soul."

Miss Cotters' wire-framed glasses were on a nearby chair with a folded sheet of notepaper addressed "To Whom It May Concern" in her old-fashioned, spidery penmanship.

Doctor Horton unfolded the note and read it. He slowly refolded it, sadly shook his head and handed it to me.

I opened the note and read, "Lachlan's banana cake is on the kitchen table."

After the War

THE DESCENDANTS OF the six Scottish families who originally settled the land west of Tools Rock still lived on their family farms. Adjoining lands were purchased as families expanded and some members moved to town, but the original farms remained central to the families' identities.

When my great-grandparents acquired their land, they built their little one-room house on a hill overlooking the surrounding rolling prairies of timber, fields and farmsteads, a view that pleased their eyes as well as the eyes of their many descendants. The little house eventually became a wash house when it was replaced by a big Foursquare with a wrap-around porch set in an expansive yard. Barns, pigpens, corncribs, chicken coops, and other outbuildings provided a backdrop.

As a kid, I enjoyed the big gatherings on the farm when relatives and neighbors congregated for plowing, haying, threshing and corn-picking. The men moved from farm to farm harvesting the hay, threshing the wheat and picking the corn. While the men worked the fields, the women cooked enormous dinners of fried chicken, pork chops, steak, mashed potatoes, cole slaw, green beans, corn on the cob, pies and cakes for the huge noontime appetites of their ravenous husbands and sons. We kids carried water jugs to the fields for the thirsty men, but mostly it was a holiday for us as we romped through our favorite haunts. Sometimes we searched the timber for blackberries, gooseberries and plums that would become pies and jams on our dinner tables. And almost always, several of us managed to slip away to Calhoun Creek for a refreshing afternoon swim.

But it wasn't only the crops that brought the families together. If someone needed a new barn or corn crib, a new roof or a paint-job, relatives and neighbors arrived to turn an otherwise long, tedious job into a day or two of good times. The women prepared dinner for the men but they also pooled their resources for canning, quilt-making, wall-papering and spring house-cleaning.

Each summer in mid-July, the MacLennan clan gathered at the farm for our family reunion. Some came from neighboring towns, and even neighboring states, but most were from the environs of Tools Rock. Everyone brought huge amounts of food which we pooled and managed to consume before the day concluded with homemade ice cream. Great-Aunt Anna expanded her collection of family gossip and chronicled the weddings, births, deaths and other notable events of the year in the family journal. And on New Year's Eve, we all descended on the farm for oyster stew, a tradition our ancestors brought from Scotland. At the stroke of midnight, we sang "Auld Lang Syne" and then piled into cars for the cold ride home over sometimes slippery snowy country roads.

Although my parents were not farmers, they joined the farm activities, partly because they grew up in such traditions and enjoyed the company of their families and partly because it allowed them to reciprocate the many eggs, hams, chickens and roasting ears we received from our country relatives throughout the year. Dad left the farm as a youth to pursue a mechanics course in Sioux City which evolved into his plumbing career. His twin brothers preferred farming and bought farms neighboring the home place. My grandfather died shortly before his youngest son Grant returned from the war. The family expected Grant to take over the family farm and that was his expectation too.

Grant was my favorite uncle. Like most men in the family, he was tall, lean, taciturn and good-looking with reddish hair and bright blue eyes. Before the war, he often drove to town, picked me up and took me to the farm for a few days. I especially remember my winter visits and the frigid, unheated upstairs rooms. When it was time for bed, Grant and I hurried up the cold stairs, quickly changed into pajamas, and jumped into the cold bed. Grant would pull me close for warmth and wrap his arms and legs around me. Some of the most secure memories of my childhood were spent sleeping in the strong arms of my uncle. He was the only person from Tools Rock I missed when I went to New York. He spent the war as a tail-gunner in the Army Air Corps, flying out of England and later Italy, and experienced some intense air battles, including two crash landings which he somehow managed to survive. When he wrote to Mom and Dad, he always included a note or a few lines for me. I responded with long letters detailing my adventures at Pine Camp. I was proud of Grant and bragged about him to all my friends. None of them had an uncle who was a tail-gunner.

One warm Sunday afternoon when I was in junior high, Grant and I were sitting on the front porch of the farmhouse eating dessert after a big family dinner.

"How many planes did you shoot down in the war?" I asked, swallowing my last bite of cake.

"Too many," said Grant. He placed his empty plate and fork on the step.

"You must've killed lots of Germans."

"I probably did."

"I told all my friends about you. When we played war games, I always pretended I was you shooting down planes and killing Germans. And in the war movies, I always imagined you were the tail-gunner."

Grant was quiet for several moments and then said, "There's nothing glamorous about war, Lach. It's a horrible thing. People do awful things to one another. I'm back home now with my family, but those men I killed aren't. That's nothing to be proud of." He picked up his plate and fork and went into the house.

It soon became apparent to me and the rest of the family that Grant had painful memories of the war he didn't want to talk about. Mom said he was still healing. Eventually, no one asked him about the war. And he never said anything about it.

AFTER THE WAR

Grant married Connie about a year after he was discharged from the Air Corps. She was an attractive young woman he met during one of his weekends in Des Moines. She wasn't Scottish and had never lived on a farm, but the family nonetheless liked her immediately. Pretty and vivacious, she was an only child and the prospect of being part of a large extended family pleased her. She immediately liked me, and fortunately I liked her, too, for I was a little jealous when I learned Grant was getting married.

Adjusting to farm life wasn't easy for Connie. Before her marriage, she had visited a farm only once. In those years, the family farm was still rather primitive, lacking electricity and indoor plumbing. But Connie tackled her new life with energy and enthusiasm. She loved Grant and was determined to create a happy life for them. The family helped her repaint and paper the downstairs of the farmhouse and her decorating skills soon had it looking better than it had in years.

Grant and Connie's daughter arrived seven months after their marriage. No one said anything about prematurity, and it was only later that I realized Connie's pregnancy was the reason for the marriage. Her mother stayed at the farm after the baby was born, and my Mom visited frequently to offer whatever assistance she could. Gradually, both older women realized something was wrong with the baby. She made few movements and rarely cried. But it was some six months later that Connie's doctor told her he thought the baby was abnormal. More doctors examined the infant and eventually they discovered that only a small portion of her brain was developed. Such a child, they said, sometimes lived several years, but

85

she would never mature beyond infancy. They strongly urged that the baby be placed in the state hospital for mentally handicapped children, and after much soul-searching and discussion with the family, Grant and Connie followed their advice. The little girl died six months later.

It was extremely difficult for both of them. After the baby was institutionalized, Connie sometimes suddenly began crying. In taciturn Scot fashion, Grant controlled his emotions but it was evident that the child's fate hurt him, too. In fact, the pain was probably greater for him because he never spoke about it, whereas Connie talked about little else if someone was around to listen.

Farming didn't go well for Grant. Although he grew up on the farm, he was still a bit green about farming. His four years in the military happened at the critical age when most young farmers learned the art and science of agriculture as they worked alongside their fathers. When Grant returned from the war, he was handed the farm and told to make it work. In addition to his inexperience, he dealt with a season of heavy rains that drowned crops. The next year brought a drought that burned them. The third year yielded bumper crops, but with accompanying low prices. Grant worked from sunup to sundown, but never seemed to get ahead.

Two years after the first baby was born, a second child arrived. This infant was a beautiful boy and everyone agreed he was exactly what the young couple needed. Now things would improve for them.

※ ※ ※

AFTER THE WAR

In September of my freshman year in high school, an early frost visited central Iowa quietly turning the trees to brilliant shades of amber and gold. Then warm weather returned, and day after day I awakened to Indian summer. I liked autumn. Something about the brilliant colors and the impending death of the countryside appealed to my sometimes-gloomy Scottish soul.

I decided against going out for football, despite considerable pressures from the coach and friends. As always Mom and Dad let me make my own decision. After reluctantly following my friends into junior high football, I decided I disliked the sport. I preferred basketball and running which allowed me to challenge my body in less brutal ways.

On a late Friday afternoon, I was waiting at home on the front porch for Grant, who'd called earlier in the week and asked me to help him with corn-picking that weekend. The crop looked promising, and Grant, like other farmers, wanted to get the corn out of the fields before the fall rains arrived. I was happy to help Grant. We were seeing less of one another, but I was still very fond of him. And I also looked forward to spending some time in the country.

When Grant drove up, I grabbed my overnight bag and walked to the car. Mom appeared at the door and called, "Hello Grant. How's everything on the farm?"

"Busy, busy. I've got a lot of corn to get in."

"How are Connie and the baby?"

"The baby's been sick with a bad cold. We took him to the doctor yesterday. I have to stop by the drugstore for some more medicine."

"I'm sorry to hear that," said Mom. "I hope he's better soon. Say 'Hello' to Connie."

"I will." As we drove away, Grant said, "I hope I'm not ruining your weekend."

"Not at all. I didn't have anything planned. What've you been up to?"

Grant sighed. "Same old stuff. Never a spare moment on the farm at this time of year. So you decided against football this year?"

"Yeah."

"Wise decision. A good way to break a few bones. I broke my collarbone in football my junior year. I can't believe you're in high school already. Soon you'll be in college."

"I guess so. And then, thanks to Miss Cotters, I'm going to do some traveling." Miss Cotters had surprised me and everyone else in Tools Rock by leaving her entire estate to me. Her only stipulation was that I graduate from college before I acquire it.

"I still can't believe she left you all that money. Did you have any idea she might do that?"

"Absolutely not. I knew she liked me. I was always nice to her, but not because I expected anything from her. That's just the way Mom and Dad raised me."

"It's certainly an incentive to go to college," said Grant. "You can only collect it if you go to college, right?"

"Right, but I'd go to college anyway."

"Whatever you do, don't try farming. Get yourself an education."

"How's farming going?"

"I'm not a farmer, Lach. I don't think I can handle the farm much longer."

"You could do other things."

"Not many. I only know how to shoot a tail-gun. Not much call for that anymore."

"You could work at Maytag."

"I'd go crazy stuck on an assembly line."

We stopped at the drugstore for the baby's medicine and then drove to the farm.

"Will you get the cows, Lach?" asked Grant, as we pulled into the driveway. "They're down in the east pasture. I've got to get this medicine to the baby. I'll meet you in the barn with the buckets. Do you still know how to milk a cow?"

"Sure thing." I opened the barnyard gate and walked toward the creek where the cows were gathered near Letha's plum tree. For the thousandth time, I thought of Letha and wondered what she would be doing if she were alive. I usually visited her tree when I was at the farm. The previous summer, I spent several hours exploring the Indian site she showed me when I was a kid. I found some shards, several arrowheads and a stone scraper.

A half-dozen mooing cows interrupted my thoughts. More than ready for milking, they cooperated when I herded them toward the barn. Inside the barn, I hooked their necks into stanchions, including old Bessie who no longer gave milk but she'd been around so long we couldn't bear sending her to the rendering works. Three cats appeared, knowing milking-time meant dinner-time for them. Grant hadn't arrived yet with the buckets so

I couldn't begin milking. I waited about ten minutes and then walked to the house to see what was keeping him. Above me a V-shaped flock of migrating geese honked their way southward. When I neared the kitchen door, I heard angry voices.

"And what do you care?" Connie shouted. "I'm the one who takes care of him all day. You always find something to do outdoors. You like this stupid farm more than you like me or the baby." She started crying.

"What can I do here?" asked Grant. "I can't make him better. There's work I gotta do. You still have no idea how much work's involved in running a farm. Do you think I enjoy working twelve hours a day?"

"Yes, I think you do. I think you do so you won't have to spend time with me. So you can come in and eat, go to bed, and get up again and leave the house. I never see you. The baby never sees you. If we disappeared from the face of the earth, you wouldn't even notice because all you ever think about is this stupid farm."

"'This stupid farm' is how we make our living."

"Some living! If I'd known I'd be stuck out here all by myself, I'd never have married you!"

"I would've had some second thoughts too if I'd known a few more things."

"I knew you didn't want to marry me." Connie started crying again.

"For Christ's sake, don't start that again!"

I decided to return to the barn. A few minutes later, Grant arrived with the buckets. He was very tense and his face flushed. "Sorry I'm late. I got held up."

That evening, after we finished the chores, we joined Connie for supper. Connie and Grant were cool toward one another, but they maintained civility in my presence.

"It's always so good to see you, Lach. Won't you have another pork chop?" said Connie.

"No, thanks. Two is plenty. I'm full."

"I hope you saved room for dessert. I baked a custard pie. I remembered it's your favorite."

"Thanks. I love custard pie."

Connie smiled and began clearing dishes from the table. She took them to the kitchen and returned with a custard pie and serving plates. As she cut the pie, I asked about the baby.

"He's sleeping a lot. The doctor said the medicine would make him sleepy."

Grant said little. When he finished his pie, he announced, "I'm going to turn in. It's been a long day. Think you can start at five in the morning, Lach?"

"If you can wake me up, I can start."

"Can't you stay and talk awhile?" asked Connie. "It's so seldom we have company."

"I'm exhausted, Connie. I've been up since four this morning."

Connie turned to me. "You can stay and talk, can't you, Lach?" she asked, almost pleadingly.

"Sure. I'm not tired."

"See you at five, Lach," Grant said. He left the room and went upstairs.

"I'm so glad you could come, Lach. You've no idea how lonely I get out here. Sometimes I don't think I can stand it another day."

"Maybe you should take a vacation and visit your mother for a while."

"I did in August. The baby almost drove Mother crazy. She doesn't care much for children. They certainly do change your life."

She sighed and looked around the room. "I hardly ever see Grant. He comes in to eat at noon and then I don't see him until evening. He eats and goes to bed. That's the way it is every day. And since the baby became sick, I'm a nervous wreck."

I couldn't think of anything to say.

"I can only get one radio station out here and it's mostly farm news," Connie continued. "I've grown to hate everything about this farm."

"There are some nice places on the farm. Maybe you should go outside and walk around more."

"Nice places? Ha! That's easy for you to say. You're not stuck out here every day. Even Tools Rock is exciting after a week out here."

"You have lots of time to read."

"I hate to read. I like to be with people. My main entertainment is listening in on the party line. Whenever the phone rings, I listen in. If I'm eating, I take my plate with me and eat while I listen. That's what my life has become."

"Maybe after the corn is in, you'll see more of Grant. The baby will be better then. Maybe you can do more things together."

"He'll find other excuses for staying away. I don't know what's wrong with him, Lach. I try to talk to him. But he never says anything. The men in your family don't know how to talk. You're the only one I can talk to."

"I'm sure things will get better," I said, not very convincingly.

"And I'm sure they'll get worse," she said, sobbing. "He doesn't even sleep with me anymore."

"I'm really sorry," I said, uncomfortably.

"He has terrible dreams. Sometimes I hear him screaming in his room. If I go in and wake him up, he won't tell me what he's dreaming. He says it's just a nightmare about the war. I don't know what to do." She continued crying.

"Maybe you should talk to Mom. She usually knows what to do."

She looked at me through her tears. "I'm sorry, Lach. I shouldn't be telling you these things. There's nothing you can do. But I've got to talk to someone." She left the room in sobs.

At five o'clock the next morning, Grant awakened me from a sound sleep. While I dressed, he fixed a big breakfast. Connie was still sleeping.

We entered the farmyard to milk the cows as a very pink dawn colored the east. We worked all morning, unable to talk above the noises of the tractor and cornpicker. At noon we returned to the house where a big meal awaited. Connie served us and then left to attend the baby. We hardly spoke as we attacked the food. After dinner, we sat in the yard under an oak tree before returning to the fields. We labored all afternoon and into the evening. It was almost dark when we milked the cows. We went to the house where Connie had supper waiting.

"How's the baby?" asked Grant.

"I think he's worse. He's coughing more."

"If he's not better in the morning, we'll take him to the doctor."

Unaccustomed to such hard work, I was exhausted. I excused myself and went upstairs, slipping into an immediate and deep sleep.

In the middle of the night, I was awakened by screams. I glanced at the illuminated clock on the bedside table. It was 3:10. A crack of light appeared under the door. I stumbled sleepily into the hallway. The sounds were coming from the baby's room.

"He's dead!" Grant cried. "He's dead!"

I ran to the open door. Connie was sitting on the bed in her bathrobe sobbing into her hands. Grant was at the crib, staring at the baby.

He then ran from the room, down the stairs and out the kitchen door.

"What happened?" I asked.

Connie looked up through her tears. "He died, Lach. He died. He was sicker than we thought."

"Where'd Grant go?"

"I don't know." She was calmer. "Maybe you better see if you can find him. Or maybe you should call the doctor. Or someone." She began crying again. "I don't know what to do."

"I'll call Mom and Dad. Then I'll look for Grant."

AFTER THE WAR

I put on my shoes and hurried downstairs, still in my pajamas. I rang the phone and awakened the sleepy night operator. After several rings, I heard Dad's voice, sleepy and alarmed. I told him the baby was dead. He said he would call Doctor Horton and come to the farm immediately.

I went to the kitchen door and saw a light in the barn. I hurried toward the light where I heard loud sobbing. I followed the sounds to a dark corner and discovered Grant lying face down in the hay. I went to him and awkwardly tried to comfort him.

"I'm sorry, Grant. I called Mom and Dad. They're coming with the doctor."

"It's my fault, Lach. It's my fault."

"No, it isn't, Grant. The baby was sick. You couldn't have helped him."

"I killed him, Lach! I killed him!"

"Oh no, Grant!"

"It's my fault. I should've left this farm long ago. I should've taken the baby to the hospital. It was me who killed him, as sure as I killed all those people in the war." He began sobbing again.

I didn't know whether to check on Connie or remain with Grant. He seemed more distraught, so I decided to stay with him. After sobbing several more minutes, he was quiet. We said nothing.

"Are you okay, Grant?"

He turned slowly and looked at me. "Is it another of my awful nightmares, Lach? Is the baby really dead?"

I was silent for several moments. "I'm sorry, Grant. The baby is dead."

He stared straight ahead and said nothing more.

I stayed with Grant until Mom and Dad arrived. We walked to the house and Mom went upstairs to comfort Connie. We were all sitting at the kitchen table when Dr. Horton arrived. He smelled of alcohol and appeared half-asleep. He went upstairs and examined the baby. After questioning Connie about the baby's illness, he announced that his cold had developed into pneumonia and he suffocated from severe congestion. As he prepared to leave, he said he would notify the undertaker. Grant simply nodded.

Connie's mother arrived several hours after the tiny corpse was taken away and Connie left with her for Des Moines. Dad and I milked the cows and slopped the hogs while Mom fed the chickens. We then took Grant home with us.

All day long, I considered what Grant said about killing the baby and decided to approach him. That evening he was sitting alone on the front porch. I joined him.

After a few minutes, I said, "Grant, it wasn't your fault the baby died."

He was silent several moments and then stood and entered the house.

The funeral was held two days later. Connie and Grant hadn't seen one another since their baby's death. During the funeral, Connie stole glances at Grant, but he stared straight ahead.

Following the service at the cemetery, the mourners returned to our house for refreshments. Grant had said nothing all day. He ate a piece of blackberry pie and drank a cup of coffee. He went outdoors and sat on the front porch steps. I joined him with my pie and coffee. We silently watched a squirrel scurry across the yard in front of us and climb into a big maple tree exploding with autumn colors.

"Gramma says if squirrels have thick coats of fur in the fall, it means we'll have a bad winter," I said, trying to make conversation.

Grant was quiet several moments and then said, "Squirrels always have thick fur in the fall, no matter how bad the winter may be." He stood and walked to his car and drove away.

We never saw him again.

Minnie Wren

MINNIE WREN WAS a skinny little woman who looked like a seedy Bird of Paradise. Her hair was orange, her eyes purple-shadowed, her thin lips a scarlet slash and her rouge round and pink on sunken cheeks. She had a hawk-like nose and beady eyes and her head bobbed when she walked. She favored bright print dresses and always sported a hat of kelly green or canary yellow decorated with a colorful cluster of fake feathers.

Minnie was one of the town characters. I came to know her during my freshman year in high school when I was the carry-out boy and shelf-stocker at the grocery store where she shopped.

Minnie lived about six miles outside Tools Rock near a turn in the highway called Bent Nest, once a tiny town but now only three houses and an abandoned gas station surrounded by cornfields. One house was home for an old retired farmer, but the others were long uninhabited with windows broken and chimneys toppled. Minnie's father owned eighty acres of farmland which he rented out to support himself and Minnie. No one ever saw the old man, but everyone saw Minnie when she came to town every Saturday for her weekly shopping and overnight stay with her ancient aunt who was Tools Rock's oldest resident. Someone once told me she was over a hundred years old, but I'm not sure that was true.

Every Saturday morning at ten o'clock, Minnie flagged down the Greyhound bus in front of the abandoned Bent Nest gas station, always paying the driver in exact change, wishing him a sweet "Good morning," and sometimes giving him gifts of homemade cookies or grape jelly. The bus dropped her off at the Sinclair gas station in Tools Rock and she walked two blocks to the Square where she bought her weekly groceries, and then walked to her aunt's house for lunch. It was rumored the ancient aunt ate nothing but cornmeal mush and bacon grease. I wondered where she got her bacon grease and decided she must eat bacon too. After lunch, the aunt took a long nap and Minnie returned uptown to the Southside Tavern, one of the few women in town who frequented the male hangout. It was a rather rowdy group; certainly no respectable man in Tools Rock was ever seen entering the tavern, at least not by the front door. The back door, however, admitted a lively array of respectable townsmen.

Each Saturday Minnie's purchases were as predictable as her arrival. When she entered the store, she always chirped, "Good morning everyone! Here it is Saturday and I'm back in town again." She was a genuinely sweet woman who generously shared her wide smile of crooked yellow teeth with everyone. I never knew Minnie's exact age, but she was probably in her mid-fifties. She braved rain, snow, ice, heat and wind, and few people could recall a Saturday morning when Minnie didn't come to town. Her trip to Tools Rock was obviously a treasured respite from the life she lived the rest of the week. She was the oldest of five siblings. The others had moved away, but Minnie remained with her parents on the little farm, cared for them in their old age and continued caring for her father after her mother died. She was unmarried, but not because she disliked men. Quite the contrary. During her weekly visits to the Southside Tavern, she enjoyed the company of numerous gentlemen admirers. Outsiders considered her a rather odd duck, but Tools Rock was accustomed to Minnie and tolerated her ways. "Poor Minnie," the townswomen would say. "She's always been a bit different. But such a kind soul to care for her old father." And they looked the other way when she entered the tavern each Saturday afternoon.

    I was too young to patronize the tavern but on Saturdays, its manager ordered groceries, so I caught glimpses of its interior when I made deliveries. Late in the afternoon, I loaded the groceries into a shopping cart and pushed it to the back door of the tavern. The greasy little kitchen was at the front, so I had to pass through the tavern, which always reeked of old smoke and stale beer and blasted country music from a brightly lighted jukebox. Invariably, I saw Minnie. She always waved and smiled hello and said I was her favorite grocery boy. Seated in a booth with a beer, a cigarette and a man or two or three, she was usually the only woman there. The men draped their arms around her and she generously laughed at their jokes. She ate supper at the tavern, often bought by one of her admirers, and as the beer emboldened the men, her admirers grew. Periodically Minnie ordered a table of dishes and invited everyone to join her, her way of reciprocating the men who treated her.

Minnie's admirers weren't exactly the cream of Tools Rock's eligible bachelors, but Minnie wasn't the choicest partridge on the bough either. She sometimes went home with one of the old bachelors, stayed the night, returned to her aunt's house in the morning and caught the one o'clock bus back to Bent Nest. Occasionally she left the tavern early and spent the evening with her old aunt listening to their favorite radio programs. No one knew what the old aunt thought of her niece's Saturday intrigues. Probably she was unaware of them since she lived in a befuddled haze most of the time.

Minnie never visited anyone in town except her aunt, but she enjoyed walking around the Square, admiring the window displays and smiling at people she met along the way. When she entered the stores, she occasionally made small purchases, but mostly she examined the merchandise. During warm weather, she sometimes rested on a bench in the Square studying the inscriptions on the big red rock. She somehow learned of each marriage, birth and death in Tools Rock, and on such occasions, she surprised many a family that hardly knew her with a note of heartfelt congratulations or sympathetic condolences. Everyone liked Minnie Wren, but no one really knew her. She was a strange one.

❧ ❧ ❧

BEFORE SUMMER

I never interacted much with Minnie beyond the store, but she was once the indirect target of one of our adolescent pranks. One Saturday night when I was a sophomore, Ross Hamilton and I were wandering the Square looking for something to liven up the quiet night. It was late and most of the town was sleeping, but the Southside Tavern was still going strong with a dozen cars parked in front. We recognized the car of old Orval Runkle, one of the town's barflies, and decided to block it. We jacked it up and placed the back axel on blocks leaving the wheels a few inches off the street. Then we hid behind the big rock and waited for the action. A few minutes before midnight, Minnie and Orval, his bulk overflowing his bib overalls, emerged from the tavern. Minnie was tipsy and giggly and Orval was downright soused as they climbed into the car. He started the engine, put it in reverse and pushed on the accelerator. Nothing happened, so he gave it more gas. Still nothing. He floored the accelerator, but the car remained stationery. They got out of the car, puzzled. Orval opened the hood and examined the engine. Meanwhile, Jed Sepp, another of Minnie's admirers, staggered from the tavern. He saw Minnie and Orval and joined them under the hood. After a few minutes, they lost interest in the problem and piled into Jed's car and turned the corner toward his house at the edge of town.

No one knew much about Minnie's domestic life—if indeed, there was much to know. She and her father lived in a little house on their land near Bent Nest. They belonged to a class in our class-conscious little town called "poor dirt farmers," meaning their farm was unproductive because of poor soil or bad farming or both. Electricity was their only claim to modernity. They pumped their water from a well, frequented an outdoor toilet and managed without a telephone and car. Everyone wondered why they didn't move to town since they no longer farmed the land, but the old man didn't take to the city ways of Tools Rock and refused to leave the house where he was born. He was a crusty old curmudgeon and I only heard of one man who came close to seeing him. The man's car overheated near Minnie's place and he stopped for water. The old man heard him at the door and threatened to shoot him if he didn't leave the property. Minnie came to the door, dithery and embarrassed, and said her father was having a bad day. She provided water but didn't invite the man inside, but his glance through the door revealed a well-scrubbed household.

Minnie kept a few chickens and a large garden. She canned the produce from her garden and the fruit from her trees for winter consumption, and stored potatoes, carrots and cabbages in her cellar. She was a hard worker. She spaded her garden each spring, planted, weeded and harvested it, mowed her lawn, and sometimes helped work the land if the tenant needed assistance during the busy seasons. She painted her house once, and one summer a neighbor watched her reshingle her roof as he drove by each day on his tractor.

Occasionally Minnie purchased additional groceries, especially during the summer canning season when she needed bulky items like sugar and vinegar. One Saturday her groceries were too heavy for her to carry to her aunt's house, so I helped her. It was only three blocks away and I enjoyed the break from the grocery store.

"So kind of you to help a weak, older woman like myself," she clucked, demurely. "You're such a strong boy."

I never knew what to say to her, but she was so eager to talk it didn't matter much that I said little.

"So now you're in high school, Lachlan. Do you like high school?"

"It's okay."

"I loved high school. I loved coming to town each day. I took the business course. Do they still offer the business course?"

"I think so."

"I planned to go to Des Moines and work in one of those tall office buildings. The last semester of my senior year, Miss Wilders, my shorthand teacher, helped me prepare job applications for businesses in Des Moines that hired young girls with business diplomas. But when it came time to go to Des Moines for an interview, I couldn't do it. I didn't want to leave home so I didn't go." She paused. "You probably think that was silly."

"No, not really."

"Now here I am, an older woman, and I've never lived anywhere but Bent Nest. But this is a good place to live and I've had a good life. And I've always had my Saturdays in Tools Rock. They're special. Always keep something special for yourself, Lachlan. That's my advice. When everything seems bad and hopeless, you can always pull-out your something special and save the day. Like my Saturdays in Tools Rock. And my gentlemen admirers."

The winter of my junior year was snowy and bitter cold. Old timers hadn't seen such a winter since the 1930s. Icy winds swept across the prairie, plummeting the temperatures below zero. Restless from the cabin-fever induced by the bitter cold, Ross and I decided to drive to Des Moines for some diversion one Friday evening. We attended an early movie and came out to a raging blizzard. There was no way we could drive back to Tools Rock, so we stayed overnight with Ross' aunt. The storm blew into the next day and it wasn't until Monday morning that we ventured back home on the recently cleared, but still icy highway. The temperature remained below zero and the road was treacherous. Long cleared sections suddenly gave way to icy patches. We were gaining speed around the Bent Nest curve when we suddenly hit a patch of ice that sent our car skidding into a snow-filled ditch. We were uninjured, but we couldn't get the car back on the road. Bent Nest's abandoned gas station was nearby so we sought its shelter while plotting our next move.

I was the first to arrive at the station. I kicked snow from the steps and pulled the door open. I started. Seated in an old chair and dusted lightly with snow, Minnie Wren was waiting for the bus. Dressed in her purple coat with her yellow hat sprouting from her orange hair, she clasped a red purse that matched her red shoes. Like an exotic hummingbird suspended in flight, she stared straight ahead. And like the frigid white fields outside, Minnie was frozen and dead.

Bobbie, Gus and Winky

I LAY IN BED on my stomach gazing at the frosty world outside. It was a bitter cold February night, one of those nights when it seemed if the temperature dropped another degree, the entire earth would shatter into tiny bits of ice. Fresh snow left a white world made whiter by a full moon creating a special sort of frigid beauty.

Earlier that night, Tools Rock won the basketball game. But I wasn't thinking so much about the game as I was the good-looking guard from the Gooseberry Point team I saw in the shower. The visiting team's locker room was closed for renovations, so both teams used the same showers. I was immune to the nude bodies of my teammates but the muscular body of the guard turned me on. He saw me checking him out and looked back at me. I wondered if he was thinking about me the way I was thinking about him. Probably not.

I was aroused by the guard, but I was tired of beating-off. After I came, I still had the same longing to be with a man. But no man was available, at least not in Tools Rock. None that interested me anyway. I heard about men who had sex with other men. In fact, I knew three of them—Bobbie Broker, Gus Reed and Winky. But they were queers. Maybe I was a queer, too. I didn't like that possibility.

Bobbie Broker was about five feet tall, maybe fifty years old and probably over two-hundred pounds, the original "Mr. Five by Five." He didn't work anywhere, kept his hair too long and always fussed around his house in an apron. People said he was a hermaphrodite and that's why he was such a sissy. Ross told me that Bobbie's sex organs were in his throat and that's why he liked to suck dicks. I wasn't sure that was true.

When his mother was alive, Bobbie visited his queer friends in Des Moines. Some of the rowdier guys in town sometimes drove up to see him and returned home with stories of wild, drunken orgies. After his mother died, high school guys sometimes visited his house for sex. I shuddered at the thought of sex with Bobbie but despite my repulsion, I was curious about the things that went on at his house and was aroused in ways that made me uncomfortable. He occasionally rented rooms to men—always outsiders—who needed a place to stay for a few weeks. Ross said if they had sex with him, they didn't have to pay rent. One of them got drunk once and beat him up. I saw him afterwards. He had a black eye and cuts on his face.

One April night I was cruising the Square with some of the guys from school. We were considering driving to Des Moines when we spotted Bobbie's car and decided to follow it. Bobbie pulled to the side of the road and stopped. Two other men were in the car. We pulled up beside them.

"Hi, Bobbie. What are you up to tonight?" asked Ray Hampers, who was driving.

"We're being followed by some naughty boys," Bobbie said coyly. "Who's with you? Do I see cute Lach MacLennan?"

I was mortified. I hadn't been enthusiastic about following Bobbie.

"Yeah. He wanted to follow you."

"Like hell," I yelled. "It was your idea." The guys in the back laughed.

"Who's with you?" asked Ray.

"Two friends from Des Moines."

One of his friends said, "What's your name, handsome?"

A man in the back said, "Keep your hands off him. He's mine."

The other one lit a cigarette and I saw his light lipstick and mascara. Jeweled rings adorned his fingers.

Ray said, "The guys in back want to go home with you, Bobbie."

"Fuck you," yelled Ross. "You're the one who wants to go home with them."

"Now boys," said Bobbie. "Don't fight over us. There's enough for all of you. Follow me home. I have some beer in the refrigerator."

"Forget it," I said to the others. "There's no way I'm going to his house."

"Count me out too," said Ross. "I gotta go home."

"Sorry, Bobbie," said Ray. "The boys are shy. See you around." He spun his wheels in the gravel and roared away.

That encounter dampened my interest in Bobbie's sex parties. If that's what queers were, I knew I wasn't a queer. I had nothing in common with Bobbie and his friends from Des Moines, except maybe a sexual preference for men. But maybe that made me queer too.

Everyone knew Gus Reed was queer. He lived in the country with his sister and brother-in-law. No one knew what was wrong with him, but he was in and out of the state mental hospital where I heard he received shock treatments because he was queer. He didn't look anything like Bobbie. If you didn't know otherwise, you'd think he was normal, unlike Bobbie who anyone would know was queer as soon as they saw him. Gus was good-looking, tall and dark. The only distracting thing about him was his eyes which always looked sort of terrified and shifty like a trapped wild animal.

Gus was in the army during the war. Some said he was discharged because he went crazy while fighting in Europe, but others said he got kicked out because he was queer. Before he went into the army, people said he was normal. After he returned from the mental hospital the first time, everyone avoided him. Sometimes he disappeared for weeks at a time. Ross said he was arrested several times in Des Moines and jailed for having sex with men. His sister always took him back. She said the war made him that way.

My only encounter with Gus was in the fall of my sophomore year in high school. His brother-in-law asked Dad to repair their broken pump. Duncan was sick with the flu, so I accompanied Dad to act as gopher. We drove out to the Reed farm where Gus greeted us. He seemed pretty normal to me, although his nervous eyes fluttered everywhere as he took deep drags on his cigarette. His eyes kept returning to my crotch. I checked to see if I'd forgotten to zip my fly. I hadn't. When his brother-in-law appeared, Gus went inside the house. The brother-in-law showed us the broken pump. It was pumping but no water was reaching the kitchen some two hundred feet away. The brother-in-law returned to the barn while Dad dismantled the pump. He sent me to the kitchen and told me to turn on the faucet and yell when water began flowing. I went to the kitchen, turned on the faucet and sat in a chair to watch it.

A few minutes later, I heard a noise behind me. I turned. Gus stood in the doorway, completely naked stroking his hard dick. I was both startled and aroused. He continued stroking while staring at my crotch and licking his lips. I was scared and embarrassed at the arousal that spread through my groin.

"You'd better put your clothes on," I said, nervously.

He said nothing, but continued masturbating, licking his lips and staring at my bulging crotch.

"Lach! Isn't the water running yet?" It was Dad coming into the back yard.

I looked at the faucet. A steady flow of water poured into the sink.

"Yes. It's running," I shouted.

Gus turned and fled upstairs. I helped Dad finish the job and we left without seeing Gus again. Two weeks later, I heard he was back in the state mental hospital.

Men turned me on, but I wasn't like Gus Reed. I wasn't crazy.

And then there was Winky. I heard about him long before I ever saw him. Everyone knew about Winky. I didn't know his real name and I'm not sure why he was called Winky. He hung out in the Square at the county courthouse in Carston. He was in his mid-forties, mentally retarded, very cross-eyed behind thick glasses, with a harelip unsuccessfully mended by surgery. He wore faded, patched bib overalls and an old baseball cap crammed over unruly hair always in need of trimming. During warm weather, he spent most of his time sitting on the park benches outside the courthouse. In cold weather, he wandered the hallways inside or sat in the courtroom if it was in session. And he spent a lot of time in the men's room where he played with dicks for a quarter.

One spring day during my freshman year, I accompanied Mom on one of her shopping trips to Carston. She parked on the Square and we parted to pursue our separate purchases. After visiting several stores, including the music store where I bought a new Andrews Sisters record, I had to pee. I crossed the street to the courthouse and found the men's room. I entered the room, turned a corner to the urinals, and saw Winky playing with an old man's dick. I immediately turned and left the room. I found a bench outside and sat. A few minutes later someone behind me said, "I'll play with your peter for a quarter." It was Winky.

I grabbed my parcels, stood and said, "No thanks." I hurried to the car and waited for Mom.

❧   ❧   ❧

BOBBIE, GUS AND WINKY

Bobbie Broker, Gus Reed and Winky. They were the men I knew who had sex with other men. But I wasn't like them. They were weird and crazy. I wasn't weird and crazy. But maybe I'd be like them when I got older. Maybe that's what happens to you if you're queer.

I stared into the cold night. An icicle cracked loose from the roof and hit the snow with a dull thud. I sighed deeply, rolled over and pulled the blanket over my head. I ached to be with a man. Of all the millions of men in the world, surely some of them were like me.

They were out there somewhere. And I was going to find them.

Ross

GIRLS USUALLY LIKED me and sometimes that created problems. It wasn't that I disliked girls. I certainly liked them as friends and I frequently found them more interesting than most guys. The problem was the crushes. If I showed interest in a girl, she invariably got a crush on me and wanted to start dating. When I didn't return her advances, she became moody and distant. I had no sexual interest in girls whatsoever. When the guys drooled over Bonnie Landers' oversized tits, I thought she looked top-heavy. When they told stories about going all the way with Rachel Danvers, I couldn't care less—unless the story included a guy I thought was good-looking, and there weren't many of them around. Occasionally someone suggested I didn't like girls, meaning I preferred guys. Then I'd have to date a girl to prove otherwise and she'd think I was interested in her and the cycle would start all over again.

The situation was different with my friend Ross who seriously discovered girls in eighth grade. He began dating in high school and I listened long hours to detailed accounts of his dates, boring to me but obviously important to him. When we were juniors, Ross fell in love with Rebecca Anderson. It was an extremely bad choice.

Rebecca was the only child of overly protective parents. Her mother drove her to school each morning and picked her up when classes ended. At ballgames, she sat with her classmates but her parents were never far away and they always managed to chaperone the parties she attended. Her mother was a meek, mousy woman and her overweight father was glum and grumpy. I never figured out how two unattractive people like them could produce such a good-looking daughter. Practically every guy in high school wanted to date Rebecca, but gave up when they discovered it was impossible to get past her parents. Ross, however, was determined.

While Ross was mooning over Rebecca, Elaine Robbins moved to Tools Rock from California. Her mother died the previous summer and she came to Tools Rock to live with her grandparents while finishing high school. She'd visited during summer vacations and we knew her from those visits. Elaine was pretty with auburn hair and dark brown eyes. Friendly to everyone, she accepted without complaint her transplantation to rural Iowa from metropolitan Los Angeles. We pestered her with questions about California and Hollywood, and were disappointed when we learned she'd never seen a movie star. The guys, of course, were crazy about her, but much to the girls' relief, she didn't seem interested in them. I liked her immediately, partly because she represented a world away from Tools Rock. She liked me, too, and we became close friends.

During noon hour, the study hall was the high school social center where students ate their lunches. I went home for lunch, but always returned early so I could spend time with my friends before afternoon classes began. Rebecca lived at the edge of town and brought her lunch. Ross lived only two blocks from school, but he brought his lunch so he could spend time with Rebecca.

One day I returned to school after lunch and found Ross sitting alone.

"Where's Rebecca?" I asked.

"She has the flu. She may be out tomorrow too."

"You'll have a chance to check out some other girls," I joked, knowing his devotion to Rebecca.

"Rebecca's the only girl I'm interested in."

"Do you think old man Anderson will ever let you have a date with her?"

He reddened with anger. "I hate that old fart. He won't let Rebecca do anything. The only time we have together is here in study hall. I don't know what I'll do when summer comes and school's out."

"Maybe you'll have a new girlfriend by then."

"Rebecca's the only girl I want. And I haven't even had a date with her yet."

I felt sorry for Ross, but I really couldn't understand his problem. He was popular and any number of girls would be happy to date him. He was about six feet tall now with blond hair and brown eyes. He was football captain and the whole nine yards—in short, the All-American boy of our high school. Granted, Rebecca was cute but she wasn't that great, especially with the complications of her overly protective parents.

Homecoming was approaching and everyone was lining up dates for the big dance in the gym following the game. One afternoon I was crossing the school yard for home when Ross shouted my name. I waited for him to catch-up.

"I got a date with Rebecca for the homecoming dance." He was ecstatic.

"Congratulations! Did old man Anderson finally decide you're not going to ravage his daughter?"

Ross' mood changed. "Her parents will be chaperoning the dance. And she has to go home with them."

"Well, at least it's a beginning. If everything goes okay, maybe they'll let her date by herself."

"Do you think so?"

"Who knows? Maybe."

The next day, I met Elaine Robbins in study hall. "Just the man I want to talk to," she said. "Let's sit over there." She led me away from the other students.

"Do you have a date for the homecoming game yet?"

"Not yet." I'd delayed asking anyone, but knew I'd have to do so soon. Several girls had let me know they were available.

"Why don't we go together?"

I looked at her in surprise. I'd never heard of a girl asking a guy for a date. They certainly gave plenty of hints, but they never came out and asked. "Well, I don't know,"

I began. My heart sank. Elaine was a good friend, and now she had a crush on me. It would be the same old problem.

"Don't worry," she said, reading my thoughts. "I haven't fallen for you. I have a proposition that'll make life easier for both of us. Are you interested?"

"Sure."

"I'm tired of these guys hanging around me all the time. They're okay, but I'm not interested in dating and going through all that stuff. And I've a feeling you feel the same way about the girls drooling over you. So why don't we start going together?"

I shrugged.

"Believe me, I haven't fallen for you. I like you a lot and if I were going to have a boyfriend in this town, I'd probably choose you. I don't think you're interested in girlfriends anyway, but that's your business. I plan to return to California after graduation and I don't want to get bogged down with a boyfriend. But I like to go to games and dances. We can go together and everyone will think we're a pair. And we won't be bothered by the others who want to go out with us."

"You got yourself a boyfriend."

"Shake, boyfriend." She held out her hand and I shook it firmly.

The next day, my romance with Elaine was the talk of the school and that was the end of my girl-problems.

The homecoming dance was the first dance I actually enjoyed. Usually I was uncomfortable pretending I was interested in my date and worrying about how I would fake the required necking afterward. But with Elaine it was different. I enjoyed dancing with her and we always found interesting things to talk about. I knew that attending high school in a small Iowa town wasn't her first choice of things to do, but she was a pragmatist and made the best of it. She planned to attend college in California and had big plans for her future that didn't include marriage for a long time. I had big plans for my future too and we had fun sharing our dreams.

Tools Rock won the ballgame and we were all in high spirits when we arrived at the gym for the dance. The music was recorded and the lights low. I'd never seen Ross so happy. It was his first real date with Rebecca, albeit hardly a private one with a gym full of students and her parents as chaperones. He danced every dance with her and they were so engrossed in one another that no guy considered cutting in.

Mr. Anderson watched Ross and Rebecca intently. He looked angry, but since that was pretty much his normal expression, it was difficult to know his feelings. Periodically he approached Rebecca and spoke to her.

About an hour into the dance, someone played a very romantic Guy Lombardo record and turned the lights lower. Couples eased closer together as they moved slowly around the floor, seeking the dark corners of the gym. Ross and Rebecca slipped into a dark recess to the right of the stage. As I was wondering what it would be like to dance with a man and why songs weren't written about men falling in love with one another, I saw Mr. Anderson on the dance floor. He was moving among the couples, obviously looking for Rebecca. He entered the recess where Ross and Rebecca disappeared. Moments later he came out leading

Rebecca by the hand, his face red and angry. She looked terrified as he pulled her through the dancers and off the floor to his wife. They left the gym.

"Old man Anderson's unhappy about something," said Elaine, watching the incident.

"Do you see Ross?"

"Here he comes."

Ross emerged from the darkened recess, embarrassed and angry. He glared around the gym and stomped toward the lobby.

"I better go talk to him," I said.

"Okay. I'll be over at the refreshments."

I found Ross in the lobby, searching for his coat in the coat rack.

"What happened?"

"That old son-of-a-bitch," he yelled, pulling his jacket from the rack. "I'd like to kill the bastard."

"What'd he do?"

"He caught me kissing Rebecca. You'd think I was trying to rape her the way he acted. He pulled her away and slapped her. He said I was a degenerate and he didn't want to ever see me with Rebecca again." He zipped his jacket and stomped toward the door.

"Where are you going?"

"Out!" he shouted, shoving the door open.

The following Monday the incident at the homecoming dance was the talk of the school, energized by Rebecca's absence. Ross was moody and wouldn't speak to anyone. That evening Elaine called Rebecca, but her mother answered and said she was sick and couldn't come to the phone.

When Rebecca returned to school two days later, she was morose and silent. At noon, her mother was waiting outside to pick her up and brought her back for afternoon classes. She was there again at four to take her home. The next day, Rebecca told Ross between classes that she could no longer stay for lunch because her father was afraid she'd spend time with him.

For the next few days, Ross was in a dark mood. He eventually told me that Mr. Anderson wouldn't let Rebecca speak to him and threatened to withdraw her from school if she did. She could no longer participate in school activities.

"He's crazy," I said. "He thinks he owns her."

"Unfortunately, he does until she's eighteen. There's nothing she can do about it. I told her to stand up to him, but she's terrified of him. She's afraid to talk to me because she knows he'll make her quit school. And she'd die if she had to leave school."

"Maybe you better get a new girlfriend."

"It's not that easy. I love Rebecca."

About a week later, our English teacher assigned group projects. We were divided into groups of four to research the life and work of a poet, and would later report the research results to the class. Elaine and I formed a group with Ross and Rebecca. After the teacher left the room, we quickly divided the project among ourselves and then, as planned, Elaine and I withdrew so Ross and Rebecca could be alone. They sat at the back of the room the entire period, seriously talking. Ross became angry and Rebecca cried several times. When the teacher returned, Rebecca was teary-eyed and Ross was furious.

During the next week, Ross became even more depressed. He missed school several days and when I called and asked what was wrong, he said he was sick. When he returned, he hardly spoke to anyone. After two days, I cornered him and insisted he tell me what was wrong.

"It's nothing I can talk about."

"I won't tell anyone," I promised. "I'm your best friend, Ross. It's better if you talk about it."

"I promised Rebecca I wouldn't."

"Is it about Rebecca?"

"Yes."

"Ross, you gotta get over this. Date some others girls. Her father's not going to change."

"That dirty son-of-a-bitch," said Ross, vehemently. "Someone should kill him."

"He probably thinks he's doing the right thing."

"He knows he's not doing the right thing. He knows perfectly well it's wrong."

I said nothing.

"You've no idea what he's doing," Ross shouted. Then he whispered, "He's . . ." He stopped. He was having trouble getting it out. "He's trying to do it to her. That's why he doesn't want anyone else near her."

"Jesus!" I said. "You don't mean he's . . . His own daughter? Are you sure? How do you know?"

"She told me. She woke up one night and he was in her

room standing beside her bed jerking-off. Another night she woke up and he was feeling her breast. She's terrified what he'll do next."

"But Jesus! That's against the law. Why doesn't she turn him in? Does her mother know?"

"She told her, but she doesn't believe her. She said she's trying to turn her against her father."

"My god! I can't believe it."

"If you'd heard Rebecca, you'd believe it. She made me promise I'd tell no one. You have to promise too."

"I promise, but what are you going to do?"

"I don't know. I'd like to kill the bastard."

A few weeks later, I was counting the minutes of a slow afternoon at the lumberyard where I now worked on Saturdays. After no business for what seemed an eternity, three customers suddenly appeared, one of them Ross. I packaged some nails and sandpaper for Mr. Vander Weel, the Baptist minister, who left saying he hoped he'd see me in church Sunday. He always said that whenever we met. I hadn't been to church since my childhood concern about being saved, but he apparently remained hopeful I'd someday return to his flock.

Ross was next but he told Mrs. Icephena Hefflefinger to go ahead because he wanted to talk to me. Mrs. Hefflefinger was the only woman in town who wore pince-nez and the last one to give up her corset, an outdated undergarment that cruelly cinched her waist and accented her already-enormous bosom. Red-faced and slightly breathless from the confines of her corset, she precariously navigated the sidewalks of Tools Rock, appearing top heavy and about to topple from her high heels. I quickly found the paint Mrs. Hefflefinger wanted and she tottered breathlessly out the door with appropriate smiles and murmurs for me and Ross.

"Your turn," I said to Ross. "What can I do for you?"

"How's it going?"

"A slow day. What are you up to?"

"Same old stuff." He avoided looking at me.

"What are you going to do tonight?"

"Haven't decided."

He'd come to see me about something, but I wasn't sure what it was. I hadn't talked to him in a week, after being rebuffed several times. I knew the Andersons were monitoring everything Rebecca did and she only saw Ross in classes. They wrote long letters to each other which Rebecca destroyed before leaving school.

I stopped making small-talk and waited for Ross to open-up. Finally, he said, "I have a favor to ask you."

"Ask away."

He paused. "Can I borrow some money from you?"

I was surprised. We'd never borrowed money from one another. He must need it badly. "Sure. How much?"

He paused again, still avoiding my eyes. "Could you loan me fifty dollars? It'll be awhile before I can pay it back."

I was taken aback. Fifty dollars was a lot of money. I thought he probably wanted a dollar or two. "I guess I could take it out of my savings account. What do you need it for?"

He paused again and then looked at me intently. "Promise you won't tell anyone?"

ROSS

"You know I can keep a secret. What's up?"

"Rebecca and I are going to elope."

I wasn't ready for that. I thought maybe he needed to make some repairs on his car.

"Are you sure that's a good idea?"

"Yes, it's the only way. We can't wait." He told me they discussed their dilemma and decided to elope. The situation at home was becoming unbearable for Rebecca. Ross had some money saved for college and he proposed they run away to Colorado where they'd get jobs and live as a married couple. When they reached eighteen, they would marry. He added, "If anything goes wrong, I won't tell anyone that you knew anything about it."

"I'm not sure it's a good idea. But if you're determined, I'll loan you the money. I won't be able to get it until Monday when the bank opens."

"That'll be soon enough. I don't want to tell you anything else in case something goes wrong. I don't want you involved in anyway."

"Whatever you say."

"Thanks, Lach," he walked toward the door and turned. "I'm lucky to have a friend like you."

I wasn't sure I was doing the right thing, but I couldn't refuse him. We'd been best friends since we were little kids.

Ross and Rebecca decided to make their escape on a Monday night in early January. He packed his few possessions and hid them in his car. He instructed Rebecca to place the things she wanted to take in the screened-in summer porch on the side of the house opposite her parents' bedroom. At midnight, Ross would pack them into his car while Rebecca kept an eye out for her parents. At 12:30, she would join him and they would drive all night to Denver.

It's unclear what went wrong. Maybe Anderson was tipped off by Rebecca's nervousness. Maybe he heard Ross drive up. Whatever the case, he found Rebecca in the living room while Ross was loading her belongings. He got his rifle and crept to the porch. He turned on the light and surprised Ross who was carrying Rebecca's portable typewriter. He pointed the gun at Ross. Ross panicked, threw the typewriter at old man Anderson and jumped him to get the gun. During the scuffle, the gun went off and shot Anderson in the calf. He picked up the gun and swung it at Ross, hitting him on the head and knocking him unconscious. He yelled at his wife to call for help while Rebecca screamed hysterically.

Old Frank Nilsson, our night watchman, was at the fire station when Anderson called. He immediately telephoned the doctor and then the sheriff's office in Carston. Doc Horton arrived first and examined Anderson's wound. The bullet had hit his calf leaving little injury. He was examining Ross' head, when two men from the sheriff's office arrived. Anderson told them he caught Ross stealing and when he tried to stop him, Ross attacked him, took his gun and shot him. When Ross' parents arrived, they learned their son was being arrested for burglary and assault with a deadly weapon. He was taken to the county jail.

This was the story that set tongues wagging in Tools Rock the next morning.

❧   ❧   ❧

ROSS

Like everyone in town, I was shocked. I couldn't believe that Ross would shoot Anderson, although I uncomfortably remembered him saying several times he'd like to kill him. Most people in town didn't believe Ross burglarized the Anderson house. No one ever heard of a burglary in Tools Rock. The Andersons were not particularly popular, but some people nonetheless sympathized with the injured man.

I tried to visit Ross in jail, but only his parents were allowed to see him. I wrote him a letter but received no reply. The following week I attended his hearing at the Carston court house. During the course of the testimony, the aborted elopement was revealed. In an outburst of anger, Ross told the judge that Anderson was molesting Rebecca. Anderson denied it vehemently and insisted the judge ask Rebecca about it. She appeared the following day, looking sick and terrified. She didn't look at Ross throughout the hearing. In a barely audible voice, she said she never told Ross any such thing and her father had never touched her. Ross was defeated. He sighed deeply and shut his eyes. He offered no further defense.

Everyone thought Anderson would drop the charges and the episode would be chalked up to teenage tomfoolery, but such was not the case. The burglary charges wouldn't hold after Rebecca admitted the elopement plot but Anderson pushed the assault charge. Ross was sentenced to a year in the state reform school for boys. I couldn't believe it. My best friend was in jail.

I wrote to Ross at the reform school and said I wanted to visit him, but he didn't answer my letters. I continued writing and about four months later he finally responded and said he'd like to see me. My mom accompanied me during the two-hour drive to the reform school.

When we arrived we were taken to a drab reception room where we waited for Ross. Mom suggested I see him alone and I concurred.

When Ross came into the room, he looked like the same old Ross except his hair was longer. Somehow, I thought he might have changed. I later learned he had changed.

"Hi," I said, standing. "It's good to see you."

He smiled and approached me. "Thanks." We sat together on the couch.

"You look good," I said.

"So do you."

There was an awkward silence. "Everything's pretty much the same in Tools Rock," I said.

"I really don't care what's happening in Tools Rock."

Another pause filled the room as I tried to think of something to talk about.

"Are you taking classes here?"

"Yes. I'll graduate high school the same time you do."

"That's great."

He looked at me and said nothing.

"You'll be able to go to college in the fall. Just like we planned."

"I'm not going to college."

"What will you do?"

"I don't know, but I'm never going back to Tools Rock. And I'm getting out of Iowa."

"Where will you go?"

He shrugged his shoulders. "Maybe California."

"What'll you do out there?"

"I don't know," he said, irritably. "How am I supposed to know?"

"I thought you might have a plan."

"Don't worry." Another long pause. "I'll pay you back the money I owe you."

"I'm not concerned about that." He said nothing, and another long pause ensued. "Mom is here. Would you like to see her?"

"No. I don't want to see anyone from Tools Rock."

I could think of nothing else to say. After another silence, he said, "I should get back to my homework. I have an exam tomorrow."

"Okay. If that's what you want."

"That's what I want." He stood and left the room. He didn't thank me for coming.

Rebecca's parents continued escorting her to and from school. She became increasingly withdrawn and hardly spoke to anyone. Once among the top students in our class, she eventually failed all her courses and withdrew from school. A few months later, a moving van with a Kansas license plate arrived at the Anderson house and loaded-up all their possessions. The Andersons followed it out of town and no one ever saw them again.

I wrote Ross several times, but received no answers. He was released a year later but he didn't return to Tools Rock. I asked his mother where he was and she tearfully told me she'd heard nothing from him since he left the reform school. He was now eighteen and on his own.

About six months later I received a letter postmarked Los Angeles with no return address. Inside was a fifty-dollar bill.

Mr. Fraser's Books

It was a Saturday afternoon in early January of my senior year in high school. I knew it was going to be a slow day at the lumberyard, so I brought a book to read. It wasn't a very good book, but it was the only somewhat interesting one I could find in the Tools Rock library, a dimly-lighted grungy room above the fire station. I read the good titles long ago and was now reading the bad ones. The school's tiny library had little to offer, so I'd pretty much exhausted the town's reserve of books. I looked up and saw Gordon Fraser, our postmaster, open the door.

I placed my book on the counter and said, "Hello, Mr. Fraser. Can I help you?"

"I need some white enamel paint, Lach. A quart should be enough."

"I can take care of that for you." I went to the backroom. When I returned with the paint, Mr. Fraser was leafing through my book.

"How do you like this book?" he asked.

"I don't, but there's not much else to read."

"Is it from the library?"

"Yes."

"That's a poor excuse for a library, isn't it? Do you like to read?"

"I love to read," I said, "but it's hard to find good books in this town."

"I'm sure it is. What do I owe you?"

I calculated the bill. Mr. Fraser paid and left.

I was gnawing at the bit to leave Tools Rock. I hadn't decided on a college yet, but I was poring through catalogues and exploring possibilities. In order to earn money for college, I worked at the lumberyard as much as possible. I was playing basketball and when that season ended, I would go out for track. I practiced long after the others stopped, not to perfect my sport but rather to dissipate the sexuality that roared through my body. My classes didn't challenge me, but I took them seriously. Each night when I went to bed, I put an X through the concluded day on my calendar.

A few days later, I stopped at the post office to pick up the mail. Mr. Fraser was behind the counter. He was in his mid-sixties, over six feet tall and very thin with receding gray hair and pale gray eyes. Soft spoken, he said little and always wore a quiet smile. His wife, Hattie, was about five feet tall, at least a hundred pounds overweight, dyed her hair bright red and talked incessantly. I always remembered the nursery rhyme "Jack Spratt" when I saw them together. They had no children.

"Did you finish that book?" Mr. Fraser asked, handing me my mail.

"Yes, I did but I don't know why. It was so bad. But once I start a book I usually finish it, even if it's bad."

Mr. Fraser chuckled quietly. "I'm that way, too." He paused. "I have a lot of books at home, Lach, and I'd be happy to loan you some if you're interested."

"I'd love that."

"If you want to stop by my house I'll show you what I have."

"That sounds great. When would be a good time?"

"I'm home almost every evening."

"How about tonight?"

"That would be fine. About seven o'clock?"

"I'll be there," I said. "Thanks a lot."

At seven o'clock, I knocked on the Frasers' front door. I liked the Fraser house, an old brick Victorian structure that sat on a large lot among tall evergreen trees. I was admiring one of its stained glass windows when Mr. Fraser opened the door.

"Good evening, Lach. Come in."

I stepped into the entry hall. Mrs. Fraser appeared from the living room.

"Hello, Lach," she said. "It's so good to see you. I understand you're playing some great basketball this season."

"Thanks. The team's doing pretty good."

"I'm surprised that a boy like you wants to look at Gordon's silly old books. I hope you don't become like him with your nose in a book all the time." She laughed. "I'm going to get back to my television program."

She waddled to the living room where I could see a flickering television. The Frasers were one of the few families in town who owned a television set. I looked at it curiously.

"My books are upstairs," said Mr. Fraser. I followed him up the open staircase to a large room at the front of the house. The walls were lined with shelves filled with books. An easy chair, a lamp, and a desk and chair were the only furniture.

I was impressed. "You have your own library! I didn't know anyone in Tools Rock had this many books."

"Take your time and choose the ones you want to read. I'm working downstairs. Come down when you finish." He left the room.

I began examining the books. They were arranged in categories labeled on the shelves. The fiction, travel and history sections caught my interest. After about thirty minutes, I narrowed my selection to three books: *The Grapes of Wrath*, *Travels in Arabia* and *The Bounty Trilogy*. I went downstairs to the living room where Mrs. Fraser was watching "I Love Lucy" and laughing loudly.

"Excuse me," I said. "Do you know where Mr. Fraser is?"

"I think he's in the basement," she said, not looking away from the television. "Go through the kitchen and you'll see the basement door." She laughed again.

I followed her directions. As I started down the basement stairs, Mr. Fraser was coming up. I stepped back into the kitchen.

"Is it okay if I borrow these three? I'll take good care of them."

"Of course. Take as many as you like. Let me see what you've chosen."

He tilted his head and looked through his bifocals. "Oh yes. We have similar taste. I hope you enjoy them."

"I'll bring them back as soon as I read them."

"There's no rush. I won't need them. You can borrow more when you finish these." He walked me to the front door, opened it and called to his wife. "Lach is leaving now, Hattie."

She called from the living room, "Bye Lach. Come back again."

"Goodbye, Mrs. Fraser." I turned to Mr. Fraser and said, "I really appreciate you letting me borrow these. I'll take good care of them."

"I'm sure you will, my boy. Enjoy them. Good night."

"Good night, Mr. Fraser."

I stayed up until two o'clock reading *The Bounty Trilogy*.

The following Monday I stopped at the post office and asked Mr. Fraser if I could return the books that evening and borrow some more. He suggested I come again at seven.

That evening when I knocked on the door, Mrs. Fraser answered. The television was blaring in the background.

"Hello, Lach." She seemed impatient. "Gordon is upstairs." She hurried back to the television as I found my way upstairs. Mr. Fraser was sitting in his easy chair reading a book.

"Good evening, Lach. Did you enjoy the books?"

"Yes, very much. I really liked *The Bounty Trilogy*."

"Isn't that a fascinating story? I like that one too. It's interesting to read the historical accounts of the mutiny and compare them to the fictional account."

"The mutiny really happened?"

"Oh yes. Pretty much the way it's described in the book."

"I'd like to visit the South Seas someday."

"Maybe you will, Lach. Did you know that one of the men who wrote *The Bounty Trilogy* was born in Colfax, just a few miles from here?"

"Really?" I said. I had no idea anyone famous lived near Tools Rock.

"Some of his family are still there. Are you ready for more books?"

"I certainly am. Do you have any books about Indians? Years ago my Aunt Letha showed me a place on the farm where Indians used to live. I always wanted to know more about them."

"I'm afraid I don't. But I'll keep an eye out for Indian books."

"Thanks." I looked around the room. "When you read all these books doesn't it make you want to visit the places you read about?"

Mr. Fraser smiled. "I don't have to go out in the world to see all those places. I can stay here in my library and visit them."

"But I want to see the real thing," I said. "I want to travel all over the world."

"You're braver than I am. When I was your age I wanted to see the world too, but I was afraid to leave home.

I thought someday I'd be brave enough to leave but I never was. I know now, of course, that I'll never leave."

"I'm going to leave. I can hardly wait."

"I hope you do, Lach, if that's what you want." Mr. Fraser's eyes roamed the room. "I feel like I've traveled the world. Each evening I decide where I want to travel. Then I find a book about that place and journey miles away from Tools Rock. I spent last night in the Sahara Desert in the mid-nineteenth century. Thanks to my books, I've seen the world and traveled through time, and I've never had to leave the comfort of my home and family and friends."

"But wouldn't you like to see the real thing?"

"I'm not sure what the real thing is. I think my books have revealed more real things to me than I would have learned if I only traveled. Besides I'm too old to travel. I shall continue traveling from my library."

"I want to travel."

"And you will, Lach. Help yourself to anything you like. I'll go on reading."

I found three more books, thanked Mr. Fraser and left.

I visited Mr. Fraser about every two weeks, selecting new titles to read and returning the ones I'd finished. One evening after our usual initial small talk, he asked me, "Do you like to read poetry, Lach?"

"I've never read a lot of poems," I admitted. "In junior high we had to memorize some and in English class we sometimes read them." I didn't want to tell him that poetry usually bored me.

"You should try more poetry, Lach. But you have to be ready for poetry. It can't be forced on you. Unfortunately, that's what usually happens in school and most young people come away with a bad taste for poetry."

I didn't say so, but that was the case with me.

"Poetry gives me so much pleasure," said Mr. Fraser. "I've always liked poetry. When I was in school, we had to memorize many poems. Most students didn't like it, but I loved it. Do you know Henry Wadsworth Longfellow?"

"I think I read one of his poems for English last year," I said, not sure I had.

"I love his poem 'The Children's Hour.'" He began reciting:

Between the dark and the daylight,
When the night is beginning to lower,
Comes a pause in the day's occupations,
That is known as the Children's Hour.

He recited the entire poem. It was very long and I didn't understand most of it.

"Isn't that a wonderful poem?"

"Yes," I said, not really sure it was.

"I love Shakespeare too. 'To be or not to be—that is the question.'" He recited the long soliloquy from *Hamlet*. I didn't know what he was talking about.

"Isn't that beautiful?"

"It's sort of hard to understand."

Mr. Fraser laughed. "Yes, it is when you hear it for the first time. I know it so well. I forget that when I first heard it, it didn't mean much to me. But I loved the sound of the language. That's the thing with poetry. The language is so beautiful. Even if you don't always understand the thoughts being expressed, you can appreciate the language. And then when you understand the thoughts, it makes the poem even more special. Here's one that's not so hard to understand. It's more modern."

He recited Robert Frost's "Stopping by Woods on a Snowy Evening."

"That's a nice poem," I said honestly. "I can see exactly what he saw when he wrote it. It's almost like looking at a picture."

"Yes, it is. But the poem has another meaning too. Some say the poet is thinking about his impending death. That's the beauty of great poetry. It can be understood at several levels. You understand it as a picture of a woods on a snowy evening. Someone my age might understand it as a man thinking about his eventual death."

"Do you read a lot of poetry?" I asked.

"I have my favorites that I read over and over. They're like old friends. I return to them when I need comfort or clarification. Like my favorite passages in books. I go back to them. They comfort me in ways I can't express."

"That's nice," I said, unable to contribute anything more profound.

Mr. Fraser smiled. "You'll appreciate poetry more as you get older." I wasn't sure about that at the time, but it turned out he was right.

About two weeks later, I returned some more of Mr. Fraser's books. Mrs. Fraser answered my knock and because it was a television station break, she visited a few minutes before telling me that Mr. Fraser was upstairs. When I entered the library, Mr. Fraser was sitting at his desk sewing a book binding with needle and thread.

"Good evening, Lach."

"Good evening, Mr. Fraser. What are you doing?"

"I'm repairing the binding on this book. It's very old. Do you like old books?"

"Yes. I like to imagine all the people who read them before me. When I see a stain on a book, I always wonder if there's a story behind it. And sometimes I find notes in books. Once I found a recipe for dill pickles. I love old books."

"Many of these books are very old. Here's my favorite." He walked to a nearby shelf and selected a volume. "This is a first edition of *Huckleberry Finn* by Mark Twain. It was published in 1884."

"You mean this is the very first one that was ever published?"

"This was one of them," said Mr. Fraser. "Of course, other copies were printed. When the world first read *Huckleberry Finn*, this is what they read. Have you ever read the book?"

"No."

"Oh, you must read it, Lach. I'm sure you'll like it. It's one of my favorite books. I've read it so many times, but each time I read it, I find something new. It speaks to old people as well as young people. Take it home and read it."

I handled the book carefully. "I'm afraid to take this one. Something might happen to it. Don't you have another copy?"

"I do, but I want you to read this one. It would please me to know that a young man is reading *Huckleberry Finn* for the first time in the first edition. I'm sure you'll treat it carefully."

"Oh, I will," I said, admiring the book.

MR. FRASER'S BOOKS

"Here's something else you might enjoy seeing." He went to the back shelf. I followed him. "This is a set of Shakespeare. Only *Othello* is missing. There's no date on them, but from what I've been able to determine, they were probably published in the early 1800s."

"Wow! That's over a hundred years ago! Where do you find all these great old books?"

"Wherever I go, I always visit used bookstores. Some of them I've written away for."

"They must be valuable."

"Maybe some of them are, but I didn't pay too much for any of them. Here's a rare one." He pulled a large volume from the shelf. "This is a book of photographs of the Civil War. It was published in a very limited edition shortly after the war ended. Some of the photos are rather gruesome."

I carefully leafed through the book.

"Here's another favorite of mine." He walked to the other side of the room and located a book. He handed it to me. "*An Outcast of the Islands* by Joseph Conrad."

"I never heard of it."

"Joseph Conrad was a popular English writer at the turn of the century. Look at the title page."

I turned to the title page. Scrawled under the author's name was "Joseph Conrad." "Is this the author's signature?" I asked.

"Yes, I think it is." Mr. Fraser smiled warmly.

"What great books you have." I looked around the room admiringly.

"They're my children. Each evening I spend time up here. I clean and mend them. I don't want to change them too much, but I like to take care of problems that might lead to further damage. Hattie thinks I'm crazy fussing with these old books all the time. I'm afraid she doesn't appreciate books."

"Have you been collecting them all your life?"

"I've always liked books, but only during the past thirty years or so have I seriously collected old ones. I must decide what to do with them after I'm gone. I'll probably give the less valuable ones to the Tools Rock library, but I'm afraid they wouldn't take proper care of the others. You go ahead and look around, Lach. Find some more books to read—and be sure you take *Huckleberry Finn*. I want to know what you think of it."

Two days after my visit, Mr. Fraser died of a heart attack at the post office. Like most of the town, I was greatly shocked and saddened by his death. I had grown very fond of the kind old man who opened the world of books to me. He was the first person I ever talked to about books and I missed our discussions in his library surrounded by his beautiful old volumes. I lay in bed the night of his death and quietly cried at the loss of my special friend.

I attended Mr. Fraser's funeral at the Methodist Church with my parents. He was well-known and well-liked in town and consequently the church was filled to capacity. Accompanied by her two sisters who were as round as she, Mrs. Fraser was draped in black and her puffy face was even puffier from crying. When we offered our condolences, she said, "Oh, Lach. Gordon was so

MR. FRASER'S BOOKS

fond of you. He thought you were such a wonderful boy." She began crying again and rolled away with her sisters.

I became caught up in the hectic whirlwind that ended the school year. I had the lead in the senior class play and as president of the class of '52, I was involved in planning the activities surrounding graduation ceremonies.

One morning about six weeks after Mr. Fraser's death, I was cleaning my room and discovered the last three books I borrowed from the old postmaster, including the first edition of *Huckleberry Finn*. I felt guilty about keeping them so long, but I was reluctant to sever my tie to Mr. Fraser. I decided to return the books immediately to his widow. It was morning and therefore a good time since television programming didn't begin until afternoon.

Within a month of Mr. Fraser's death, Mrs. Fraser bought a little box-like house in the new residential addition of Tools Rock. I knocked on the door of the little square house and remembered my preference for the rambling old Victorian house which was currently empty with a "For Sale" sign in the front yard. Mrs. Fraser wore a bathrobe when she answered the door.

"Hello, Lach," she said. "I just finished baking a cake. Won't you come in and have a piece?"

I could see the television set. It was tuned to a test pattern. "No, thank you, Mrs. Fraser. I can't stay. I wanted to return these books I borrowed from Mr. Fraser. I'm sorry I kept them so long, but I forgot about them."

"Oh dear," she said, dismayed. "More of those old books. I sent them all to the dump. I never liked those books and I had no place for them in this house."

"You sent them to the dump?" I asked in disbelief.

"I kept a few of the new ones for my mother's little bookcase. Do you want to see them?"

"But the others all went to the dump?"

"They were old and worn. Some of them were over a hundred years old! Can you imagine keeping books like that? Many of them were falling apart."

I looked at the books in my hand.

"You can keep those books. I have no place for them."

"Thank you. I'd like to. It was nice seeing you again, Mrs. Fraser. Bye."

"Goodbye, Lach. Stop by and see me again."

I couldn't believe she had thrown away all of Mr. Fraser's beautiful old books. I decided to drive to the dump on the chance they'd been saved. When I reached the abandoned coal mine south of town that served as Tools Rock's dump, old Loud Fry was on duty. The town hired him a couple days a week to maintain a semblance of order to the dump. When I arrived he was raking up stray papers and throwing them on a smoldering fire.

"Hi, Loud."

"Lach MacLennan. What brings you out here?" He stopped raking and leaned on his rake.

"I was wondering if any of those books Mrs. Fraser threw away are still around."

"There they are." He pointed to the smoldering fire. "Just finished burning the last batch. Took a while. There was a heap of 'em."

My heart sank. I feared the books would be gone, but nonetheless I'd hoped otherwise. I walked to the smoldering pile and looked at the few pages blowing in the light breeze. I reached down and picked-up one of them. It was the title page of *An Outcast of the Islands* with the signature of Joseph Conrad that Mr. Fraser treasured so much.

"Did you want those old books, Lach?"

"Yeah, I would've liked some of them."

"Wish I'd known that. Took me forever to burn 'em. Would've been a hell of a lot easier to give 'em to you."

"Yeah, I guess so. Well, I gotta get back to town, Loud. I'll see you later." I carefully rolled up the Conrad title page and slipped it into my shirt pocket.

As I walked to the car, I thought I heard Mr. Fraser weeping.

College

MOM AND DAD drove me to campus and helped me move into the dorm room I would share with a still unknown roommate. They departed after a tearful kiss from Mom and a stiff handshake from Dad and after they left, I realized my relationship with them was changed forever. With that realization came a great sense of freedom. College was my life now. I visited the campus the previous spring and liked it immediately. Located in a small town on a bend in the Cedar River, the red brick buildings of the campus clustered around a campanile that chimed morning, noon and evening. After tiny Tools Rock High School, the two thousand students were somewhat intimidating but nonetheless exciting.

I found a job my second week on campus. I saw an ad in the student newspaper for a proofreader and decided to apply for it. After locating the newspaper offices on the top floor of the oldest building on campus, I was greeted by a tall thin blond woman dressed in black with a huge orange purse slung over her shoulder. She identified herself as the editor.

"What year are you?" she asked, retrieving a cigarette from an overflowing ashtray.

"Freshman."

"Upper classmen are usually better qualified for this job." She looked me over and blew smoke through her nose. "But if you want to take the test, be my guest."

"I'd like to try it. I really need a job." I looked up and saw a banner stretched across the wall above her desk demanding in large black letters: "Abandon Hope All Ye Who Enter Here."

"You have to be a little crazy to work here," she said, glancing at the banner.

"I can probably manage it."

"Okay, let's go for it."

She led me to a small room, gave me two pages of copy and left. Filled with spelling, punctuation and grammatical errors, the copy was about the previous spring's commencement ceremonies. I easily corrected it, returned to the office and handed the copy to the slim blond woman in black.

"You're fast if nothing else. I'm Es. Es Stevens."

"I'm Lach. Lach MacLennan."

"Leave your phone number and I'll let you know if you get the job. We're accepting applications until Friday noon."

I wrote my name and phone number on a slip of paper, thanked her and left.

After a Coke at the student union, I returned to the dorm and discovered my roommate had moved in. He was a chubby chemistry major and seemed disappointed when I told him I would probably major in English. I was hoping for a different sort of roommate, preferably a good-looking hunky guy who shared my sexual appetite. But I knew that was unlikely. This guy seemed a quiet studious type so he would probably work out.

The next day after lunch I was resting in my room before my next class when the bell above the door announced I had a telephone call. I ran to the phone at the end of the hall.

"Is this Lach MacLennan?" asked a voice on the phone.

"Yes it is."

"This is Es. Do you still want the proof-reading job?"

"I sure do."

"It's yours. Can you come by tomorrow?"

"Sure," I said, quickly thinking through my class schedule. "How about one o'clock?"

"Great. See you then." I sauntered back to my room, whistling "The Boogie Woogie Bugle Boy." I hadn't expected to find a job so soon. The pay wasn't great, but it would keep me in pocket money.

One evening several weeks later, I was studying in the library. I went to the men's room and saw written on the wall above the urinal "Blow job in stall behind you." I looked behind me, but the stall was empty. I finished peeing and entered the stall. The walls were covered with drawings of cartoon characters with big dicks engaged in all sorts of sexual antics. "Meet here at 9 p.m. 10/7 for great blow job" was scribbled on the back of the door.

I was intrigued and aroused at the prospect of meeting someone who shared my sexual interests. I glanced at my

COLLEGE

watch. It was eight o'clock and it was October 7. I decided to come back at nine.

I returned to the study room, but couldn't concentrate. I watched the clock. Finally, it was five minutes before nine.

When I entered the restroom, someone occupied the stall where the message was scrawled. I went into the adjoining one and sat down. Under the partition, I could see the foot of the person in the neighboring stall. It began slowly moving up and down and then stopped. Moments later it moved again, this time inching toward my foot. I didn't know what I was supposed to do. The foot tapped again and inched closer to mine until it made contact.

"Let's go outside and talk," I said.

The man next to me suddenly withdrew his foot, pulled up his trousers and rushed from the restroom before I could see him. He obviously wasn't interested in talking. I returned to my books, puzzled by his behavior.

The job at the newspaper worked out well for me. It provided the money I needed to supplement my savings and the staff provided friends. I liked journalistic writing and I liked the excitement of putting a paper out every week.

Equally exciting were the classes I was taking. In high school I was a serious student but always felt very much in the minority. But at college I discovered students who shared my enthusiasm for learning. My classes were run-of-the-mill freshman introductory courses, but they opened great vistas to me. I'd never heard of *The Iliad* and was amazed to discover it'd been around for centuries.

Machiavelli's philosophy was familiar but the man wasn't. A music appreciation course explored classical music and an art class gave me hands-on experience in a variety of media. My French class was taught by an elderly German man who delivered a tirade against Hitler each week and insisted we sing "Les Marseilles" at the beginning of each class. I still know all the lyrics.

About a week after my exploration of sex in the library restroom, I decided to give it another try. I entered the stall where the earlier message appeared. The drawings were washed from the wall, but beneath the tissue paper holder, a message in very small letters appeared: "8 p.m., Mon. Wed., blow job, here." I decided to check it out the following night.

I arrived early so I could see who left the message, but someone was already in the stall. I entered the adjoining one and sat down. Again, the foot next to me, larger than the last one, began tapping. This time I tapped my foot. The foot tapped again and moved closer. I moved my foot. A hand reached under the partition and touched my calf. "Let's go have a cup of coffee," I said. "We can talk."

The man next to me stood, pulled up his pants and rushed from the stall. I opened the door as a middle-aged man threw me a terrified glance and fled the restroom. I walked back to the dorm. I decided I wasn't going to meet the kind of man I wanted in the library restroom.

About midway through the semester, fraternities began their search for freshman pledges. I only vaguely understood what fraternities were all about. Three of them courted me. I attended the smokers and found

COLLEGE

them incredibly dull and was soon turned off by the vapid criteria they used for selecting new members. I passed inspection at all three smokers and was invited for the second rounds.

One night I was drying in the shower room when an upperclassman came in, a football player from the least desirable of the smokers I attended.

"Hi there, Lon," he said, whipping off his towel and hanging it on a hook. "Good to see you again." He had one of those little circumcised dicks that looks like a pink rosebud emerging from a briar patch. He checked out my crotch and extended his hand.

I shook his hand and said, "My name's Lach."

"Lach, oh yeah. Funny name. Sounds foreign. Are we going to see you at the next smoker?"

"I'm not sure."

"I hope so. You seem like our kind of man. Are you a phys ed major?"

"No. I'm majoring in English."

"English? I don't think we have any English majors. You don't seem like one of them."

"What's 'one of them'?"

"You know the way they are." He put his hand out and waved it limply as he batted his eyes.

"No I don't know, but I think I know the way you are."

"What d'ya mean?"

"Think about it." I wrapped my towel around my waist and left the showers. On the way to my room, I made my decision about fraternities. They weren't for me.

❦   ❦   ❦

I stayed away from the library restroom for about a month. I was still eager to meet some men who shared my sexual interests, but I was turned off by the ones who apparently frequented the restroom. But surely there were others like me on campus. And if so, they'd probably check out the restroom the way I did. I decided to give it another try.

It was a little after seven on a Tuesday evening. When I entered someone was in the stall and a man stood at the urinal. I went into the adjoining stall. After the man at the urinal left, the foot next to me began tapping. I tapped back. The other foot responded and moved closer. I moved my foot. The other foot stopped tapping. A piece of toilet tissue appeared under the partition. I took it. On it was written, "What do you like?"

I wrote beneath it, "I'd like to talk to you. Let's go have a cup of coffee." I passed the note under the partition.

Moments later, another piece of paper appeared. It read, "I'm here to suck dicks, not socialize."

I stood, pulled up my pants and left the restroom, both aroused and disgusted.

I loved the library. I studied there, sometimes wandering its stacks, examining the rows and rows of books. No matter how bad my day, I always felt better when I entered the library, a place of respite, a place to escape to any world I chose. I liked to browse through the card catalogue. I checked to see if any MacLennans had written books. Sure enough, one had, but it was back in the Nineteenth Century. I wondered if someday someone would browse a library card catalogue and find the name "MacLennan, Lachlan Grant."

One rainy November afternoon, I was browsing the card catalogue and found "Homosexuality." The library had two books on the subject and both were marked "Restricted." I didn't know what that meant. I copied down the call numbers and went to the stacks. Neither of the books was on the shelves. I went to the circulation desk and gave the call numbers to the student on duty and asked if the books were checked out.

She looked at the numbers and said, "These books are restricted. You have to sign for them. Miss Miller is in charge of them."

"Why do I have to sign?"

"It's probably the subject matter. Some subjects aren't allowed to circulate. What are they about? Communism?"

"Yeah," I lied. "That's okay. I don't really need them. I was just curious." I returned to the reading room.

I hate myself when I lie. The more I thought about the books, the angrier I became. Why should I need special permission to read about homosexuality or communism? I returned to the circulation desk. The same student was on duty.

"I decided I want these books," I gave her the call numbers.

"I'll call Miss Miller." She returned from the back office moments later with a plump, middle-aged woman. She looked at the call numbers and then looked at me.

"Why do you want these books?" she asked, coldly. "Are you writing a term paper?"

"Yes . . ." I began. Then I said, "No, I'm not. I want to read them. Isn't that why they're here?"

She gave me a withering look and said, "One minute." She went into the back room and returned minutes later with the two volumes. "You must sign for them." She wrote the titles on a form and passed it to me. I signed the form and returned it to her.

"You must read them here in the library. They cannot be checked out." She handed the books to me.

I took the books to the reading room. The first one was an anthology of essays on homosexuality written by various "experts." I scanned the essays. They variously concurred that homosexuals were perverts, menaces to society and sinners in the eyes of God. Their remedies to the homosexual "problem" included committing them to mental institutions, castrating them and changing them to normal heterosexuals through psychotherapy and shock treatment. The second book was a slim volume by a psychiatrist. It was the most compassionate, but it concluded that without treatment most homosexuals were dangerous and potential threats to children.

I stared out the window. The day had become grayer and rain was still falling. By now I was certain I was a homosexual. I once thought I'd change as I got older and find girls sexually appealing. But I knew that wasn't going to happen. My attraction to men was becoming greater. But I wasn't a pervert. Maybe some homosexuals were, but I wasn't. Some heterosexuals were perverts, but not all of them. So why not the same for homosexuals? A menace to children? That one I didn't get at all. I liked kids but it had nothing to do with sex. It was men I found attractive.

Big strong men with hairy chests, scratchy beards and big dicks. Certainly not little kids.

I returned the books to the circulation desk, left the library and walked to the dorm in the lightly falling rain. I realized I wasn't going to learn much about my sexuality at the library.

Initially I went to the newspaper office only on Thursday afternoon to proofread the galleys of the paper that came out on Friday. But as I became acquainted with the staff, I stopped by during the week and sometimes the weekend. Before long I was taking on other duties, and I occasionally covered stories when no one else was available.

I liked the newspaper people. They weren't exactly crazy, as Es suggested, but most were a bit off-beat. I especially liked Es. She always wore black and carried a gigantic purse of rotating colors. She was dedicated to the newspaper and took only a few classes each semester so she could spend her hours on the paper. She loved to tackle controversial issues. When I told her about the restricted books at the library, she discovered a cause. I later learned that she also surmised I was homosexual, but she never mentioned it. She wrote an editorial condemning the library policy. When the paper's advisor told her to back off the issue, she attacked it more vigorously and published a list of the restricted books. It would be several years before the practice ended, but she made a lot of people aware of the library's attempt to intimidate students who wanted to read controversial books.

❖   ❖   ❖

BEFORE SUMMER

In mid-November, Es arranged a poetry-reading session for her friends. I was invited. It began at eleven o'clock on a Friday night during full moon on the flat roof outside Es' office window. Each person brought a favorite poem to share with the others. Es provided beer. As the guests arrived, she passed out beer and directed us through the window to the roof where we sat silently in a circle awaiting the others. She was breaking several college rules. The offices were supposed to be vacated at ten p.m. and the night watchman made it clear several times that the roof was off-limits. Drinking was not allowed on campus and most of us were underage.

Es followed the last person out, dressed in her usual black and carrying a huge purple purse, heavier than usual with its cargo of beer. She sat in the circle of nine and read her selection, "The Hound of Heaven." Following a five-minute silence during which we contemplated the poem, the next person read "After Apple-Picking." Five minutes later another person read and then another. Es quietly interrupted half-way through to replenish our beer. I read "The Love Song of J. Alfred Prufrock," a poem I recently discovered and only partly understood. After the final reading, we sat quietly until Es ushered us back into the office. No one spoke as we parted and went our separate ways.

I was enchanted. This was how I hoped college would be.

Rain

I RETURNED HOME TO Tools Rock each summer during college because I was assured a job at the lumberyard. I delivered orders, unloaded lumber from the railcars and occasionally helped out at the counter. It was hard physical work at times, but I didn't mind. I liked to exert my body. I started at seven in the morning and sometimes didn't get home until ten hours later. After supper I went upstairs to my room and read until Mom called me to join her and Dad for dessert on the front porch.

I felt detached from the town and my family. Duncan was married and a partner in Dad's plumbing business. My sister Maggie was already in high school and totally engrossed with her teenage friends.

If I had my druthers, I'd be elsewhere, but I cut expenses by living at home. I made good money and worked extra hours to make it even better. Tools Rock was more bearable now that I was only a summer visitor. The summers were interludes in my life. I knew the time would soon come when I'd seldom visit Tools Rock.

BEFORE SUMMER

I felt rather worldly after two years of college and interaction with the locals who didn't share my new sophistication was tedious. All they talked about was the past and the weather, never about books. The highlight of the past was their high school days and the all-consuming weather topic was the rain, or the lack of it. A drought hit central Iowa that summer. Every conversation began with speculation about the weather—how dry it was, when there was last such a drought and how many more days the crops could tolerate no rain. I didn't give a damn about any of it. My concerns were worldlier.

I was unloading lumber at the old Campbell place west of town.

"Don't look like we'll be gettin' no rain today," observed Seth Campbell, squinting up at the hot July sun. "Don't know what we'll do if rain don't come soon. Calhoun Crick's dry as a bone."

If I hear about the friggin' drought one more time, I'll scream, I thought to myself. "It's been a pretty dry summer alright," I said aloud, pulling the last two-by-four from the bed of the truck. "What are you going to build out here?"

"Corn crib. Seems a waste though. Looks like there won't be no corn if it don't rain."

"Surely it'll rain soon," I said, handing him an envelope. "Here's your bill."

"Thanks, son. Tell Keith I'll stop by and pay him the next time I'm in town. You're one of Ian MacLennan's boys, ain't ya?"

"Yes, I am. The younger one."

"Your dad and me used to run around together when

we was kids. Them was some good times we had. Best fun I guess I ever had. I don't suppose you remember your Aunt Letha."

"I certainly do. I remember her very well."

"Good lookin' woman she was. I tried courtin' her, but could never get to first base. I even carved our names on the big rock in the Square. I wonder if she ever knew that." He paused momentarily. "Sometimes I wonder how it would've been if I'd married her. Maybe she'd still be alive if she stayed here and married me."

Better she died young in Chicago than stuck out here in the sticks with you, I thought to myself.

"But you can't change the past, can you? That's what I always say."

Real profound, I internalized and then said, "That's right. I gotta get back to town. Good luck on your corn crib."

"Yeah. Don't know why I'm botherin' to build it. Corn's gonna be ruined. No rain in sight."

I climbed into the truck, turned the ignition, shifted gears and slowly drove down the rutted driveway to the gravel road where I left a cloud of dust in my wake settling on the nearby cornfields. I hadn't realized old Seth Campbell was Letha's age. He looked twice that old. Good wholesome country living.

I turned onto the highway and headed back toward Tools Rock. I looked at my watch. Time for one more run. Then I'd be done for another day and could escape to read in my room. Maybe I'd receive a letter from Es today. Maybe I'd finish *Madame Bovary* tonight.

※ ※ ※

Two days later, I was working the counter at the lumberyard. It was another slow day. Keith took the afternoon off and asked me to man the office. I preferred delivering lumber or working in the yard, but it was a hot day and it was nice to kick back and do nothing. I was reading the local paper and considering the dreary lives it chronicled when Cornie Van de Wilt came in. I hadn't seen him since we graduated from high school.

"Hey, Lach," he said. "Good to see you." He extended his hand.

I shook his beefy hand and said, "Good to see you, Cornie. How are you?"

"Think we'll get some rain one of these days?"

"I'm sure we will." I braced for yet another discussion of the drought. "It always comes sooner or later"

"I don't know. The corn's lookin' terrible. You should see that bottomland of mine. Big cracks in the ground. This is serious."

"Yeah, it's pretty bad."

"You're goin' to college now, ain't ya?"

"That's right. I start my third year this fall." And it can't come soon enough.

"Do you like that college life?"

"Yes, I do."

"You always was the brainy one in the class."

And you always were the brainless one, I remembered but said aloud, "I always liked school."

"Not me. I hated school, but I had some good times during those years. Did you know I'm married?"

"That's what I heard. Harriet Rosland, right?"

"Yep. We got married a week after graduation. Had to hurry, you know." He winked. "Couldn't keep away from that girl."

I could think of few things more revolting than Cornie and Harriet fornicating.

"I manage to keep her in the family way all the time. We're expecting our third one in the fall."

"You do keep busy."

"The first one came a little early, if you know what I mean." He winked again.

I offered an appropriate chuckle.

"Sometimes I miss high school. I remember my mom tellin' me them would be the best years of my life. I think she was right. We really had some good times, didn't we?"

"Yeah, we really did." I couldn't think of a single good time I had with him.

"I need some shingles for the barn. Don't know why I'm botherin' though. I don't think it's ever gonna rain again. I never seen it so dry."

After Cornie left, I walked a half-block to buy a Coke at the Southside Tavern. Following the inevitable comments about the drought, I returned to the lumberyard. Euela Fraken was waiting at the counter.

"Hello, Mrs. Fraken," I said slipping behind the counter. "Sorry to keep you waiting. I went out for a Coke."

"That's alright," she said, smiling sweetly. Her smile was always too sweet. "You gotta do somethin' to beat this heat. I'm afraid it's never gonna rain again."

"I'm sure it'll rain one of these days. What can I do for you?"

"I need about seven feet of screen wire. Our kitchen door's got holes in it and I'm gittin' tired of swattin' the flies."

I unrolled and measured the screen wire. Mrs. Fraken watched and said, "You've grown into such a nice lookin' young man, Lach."

When people told me that, I always wondered if I'd been a really ugly little kid. "Thank you, Mrs. Fraken. How's everything with your family?"

"Fair to middlin.' Waitin' for the rain. Mary's home this summer. You should stop by and see her. You'd have lots of college stories to swap."

And I'd have to dodge her tits. Mary Fraken was the first girl in class to get tits and with them came an overactive sex drive. She always managed to corner the boys and shove her tits into them. She had an eye for their crotches, too.

"Does Mary like college?" I remembered she was attending some Bible-thumping school in Missouri.

"She loves it. Gets straight A's. She's decided to become a missionary."

I almost choked. Nympho-Mary a missionary! I could hardly keep a straight face. She's probably after those naked men in the *National Geographic* magazines.

"That reminds me," continued Mrs. Fraken. "This Sunday evenin' the Baptists and Methodists are havin' special prayer meetins for rain. We'd love to see some of your family there."

"We're not church people," I said, thinking a mask and rattle would probably bring the rain sooner than their prayers. I tied the screen wire into a roll and placed it on the counter.

"But this is special. We need all the prayers we can get to end this awful drought."

"I'll tell my parents."

Mrs. Fraken paid for the screen wire. As she left, she shook her head sadly, "I don't know what we'll do if it don't rain soon."

The late evening desserts with Mom and Dad on the front porch were pleasant conclusions to the summer days. Occasionally Maggie joined us, but she was usually out with her friends. Sometimes neighbors or relatives stopped by to chat but typically it was only the three of us talking as we watched fireflies punctuate the night with flashes of light. Our conversations inevitably began with the drought and then moved into family affairs, often speculation about what happened to Grant and whether we would ever see him again. The family had tried to locate him, even hired a private detective, without success. Mom and Dad sometimes reminisced about their rural childhoods, the tough times of the Depression and our years in New York.

One evening during a pause in conversation, Dad said, "What do you think you'll do after college, son?" He was sitting in the porch swing with Mom.

I didn't hesitate. "First, I'm going to travel. I'm going to take off and see the world."

"And after you get that out of your system, then what?"

I thought a moment. "I really don't know yet." I paused. "I think I'd like to write. I'd like to have a job where I can write."

"Where do you want to live?"

"Anywhere but Tools Rock." I quickly added, "I don't mean that the way it sounds. Tools Rock's a great place for people who fit in. But I've never fit in. I've never felt like I really belong here."

A small silence filled the porch.

"Your Dad and I have always known that, Lach," said Mom. "We've always known you were special and would someday leave Tools Rock. We wish you didn't have to, but we love you and want you to be happy." That was the closest my parents ever came to acknowledging my homosexuality. But that was enough; there wasn't need for anymore.

A car rounded the corner and stopped in front of the house. It was Duncan. He bounded out and sat on the porch steps beside me.

"How's it going, Dunc?" I said, clapping him on the shoulder.

"Okay," he said, reaching over and squeezing my knee. "I was talking to Wayne Cameron up at the drugstore about the drought."

Surprise, surprise I said to myself.

"Everyone's feeling it," said Dad. "Farmers are putting off plumbing jobs because they don't know what the harvest's going to be like."

"The business is really hurting," added Duncan. "I was hoping to trade my Chevy in for something newer this summer, but I guess I'll keep patching it up. Diane was hoping for a new dinette set, too. The way things are going, we'll be lucky if we can pay the rent."

"You know your Dad and I will help you if things reach that point," said Mom.

"Thanks Mom. I know, but I hope it doesn't come to that."

I looked at Duncan's profile. He had matured into a good-looking man. I'd never considered his looks before. He was always just my older brother who gave me a hard time when we were kids. The bright red hair of his youth had turned a deep copper, but he still had his sparkling blue eyes. Too bad he couldn't get out of this one-horse town and do something with his life.

"How are things at the lumberyard?" he asked.

"Not bad. A bit slow at times, but I keep busy."

"Are you still working long hours?"

"Yeah. I need the money."

"I'm surprised Keith's giving you all those hours. He told me business was really down."

"I think he knows Lach needs the money for school," said Dad.

I'd never considered that.

"Well, I better get home," Duncan said, standing up. "Good seeing you, Lach. See you in the morning, Dad. Bye, Mom."

After he left, Mom said, "I feel sorry for Duncan. This drought has really cut into his earnings. With a wife and new baby, he needs all he can make. We can fall back on savings, but he doesn't have any."

"Surely it'll rain soon," said Dad, "and things'll get back to normal."

"I hope so," Mom added, looking up into the clear starry sky. "But it doesn't look too promising tonight."

The prayer meetings were held at the local churches, but the heavens were disinclined to help the farmers. No rain came. I became less cynical as the drought worsened. I offered to cut back my hours at the lumberyard after learning Keith was keeping me on because he knew I needed the money for college.

"No need for that, Lach," he said. "There're plenty of things you can do around here. We got to keep you in college so you can make us proud of you. We're expecting great things from you."

"Thanks, Keith. I hope I don't disappoint you."

"I know you won't, son."

A gloom settled over Tools Rock and the surrounding countryside as people resigned themselves to ruined crops. The old farmers said they'd seen nothing like it since the awful droughts of the Depression years. The younger ones wondered how they'd make it through the year if rain didn't come soon. I increasingly realized the severity of the drought. I insisted Keith cut back my hours since there was nothing for me to do at the yard most of the time. Reluctantly, he agreed.

It was a hot Wednesday of the second week in July. The lumberyard was unusually busy and I worked a full eight hours, the first time in over a week. I walked home that evening, exhausted from the long day's heat. After supper, I escaped upstairs to read in front of my fan. I began dozing. I looked at the clock. It was only nine.

RAIN

I tried reading again, and then decided to stop fighting sleep. I doused my light and within minutes fell asleep.

About two a.m., I was awakened by a great crack of thunder that shook the house. I sat up in bed, startled, and looked out the open window. A light breeze blew the curtain. It was decidedly cooler. Another crack of thunder sounded through the darkness, and the eastern sky glowed with sheet lightning. Drops of rain splattered against the window. I heard Mom and Dad downstairs and hurried down to join them.

"It's raining, Lach! It's finally raining!" Mom wore her bathrobe. Her face was radiant.

Dad, in pajamas, peered out the front door excitedly: "Looks like it's going to be a real gully-washer!"

Maggie came downstairs, sleepy and smiling: "It's rain! It's really raining!"

We went outside on the front porch and watched the rain fall in torrents.

"It's beautiful," beamed Mom. "It's so beautiful." She walked down the steps and stood on the sidewalk, holding her arms to the rain.

"You're getting soaked, Eliza," said Dad.

"Who cares?"

Maggie and I joined her on the sidewalk, laughing and splashing in the puddles.

"C'mon, Dad!" said Maggie.

"You're all crazy," he said, reluctantly joining us.

"Look, the Shafers are out too," said Mom. Across the street our neighbors stood in the rain laughing and shouting at us.

I looked up and down the street. Lights were on and everyone was in the street, yelling and laughing. Kids danced and splashed in the puddles while dogs barked and romped among them.

"Whole damn town's gone crazy," said Dad, happily.

"What a wonderful way to go crazy," laughed Mom. She grabbed Dad and they danced down the street in the pouring rain. I'd never seen them dance before. Maggie took my hand and we skipped behind them. The pajama-clad Boyd brothers bicycled among the revelers, making wheelies on the slick street. Uptown, the bells of the Methodist church began pealing, and not to be outdone, the Baptists added their more somber notes to the celebration. The two a.m. Rock Island freight train lumbered through town contributing its mournful whistle to the festivities. A few blocks away, some leftover Fourth of July firecrackers exploded, competing with the thunder and awakening several roosters who offered their raucous cries to the rainy, jubilant night.

We talked and shouted and laughed with neighbors as the rain poured, the thunder sounded and lightning illuminated the sky. When thoroughly soaked, we reluctantly went indoors, found towels and put on dry night clothes. I climbed upstairs to my room and lay in bed watching the rain flow from the roof, soak the thirsty lawn and rush down the street in rivulets.

The crops of Tools Rock were saved.

I smiled with great relief, rolled over and slowly fell asleep to the comforting sounds of the nourishing rain.

Wolf on the Prowl

"JESUS, MAN! YOU'LL get a hernia carrying around that basket."

I was toweling myself dry in the dormitory shower room. I looked up and smiled at the skinny guy across the room.

"I'm your neighbor," he said, wrapping his towel around his waist. "My name's Wolf." He stretched out his hand for a shake.

I shook it and said, "I'm Lach."

"Lock? As in key?"

"No. Lach as in Lachlan. Wolf as in predator?"

"Yeah. I'm preying on all the little minds around here that need opened. Charles Wolfington, but call me Wolf."

"Wolf it is," I said. "Are you new on campus?"

"Yeah. Transferred from Podunk U. I'm hoping for big things here, but so far I'm disappointed."

"What kind of things?" We left the shower room and walked down the hall.

"People who aren't afraid of ideas, people who know something about art. Interesting people like atheists, whores, drunks and perverts. So far I've met nothing but farmers and jockstraps. Which one are you?"

"You'll have to figure that out. I'm still working on it." I stopped at my door. "This is my room."

Wolf stopped at the door across the hall. "And this is mine. I got scotch and vodka inside. Care for a nightcap?"

"I'll take a rain check. I got a test tomorrow."

"Serious student. Too many of your kind around here." He entered his room and closed the door.

Two nights later, I returned to the dorm from the library where I was working on a paper for my Victorian lit class. As I inserted my key in the lock, the door across the hall opened.

"Hi Lach as in Lachlan. What's up?" It was Wolf.

"Hi. I just got back from the library."

"Communing with the campus intellects? I heard they all met in the elevator tonight."

I smiled and said, "Where you off to?"

"Over to The Walrus for a nightcap or two or three or four. Care to join me?"

"Sure," I said after a slight pause. I was tired of studying and not yet ready for sleep. The Walrus was the unlikely name of a local bar that catered to students. "Think they'll be checking IDs tonight?"

"You don't have a fake one yet?"

"No. I've only got six months to go."

"That's beside the point. Beating the system is what it's all about."

I tossed my books onto my bed, closed the door and joined Wolf. "You look like you ran into a paint truck," I said, appraising his paint-spattered jeans and sweatshirt. "Are you an art major?"

"I'm not bound by any dumb-ass university categories. I'm trying to expand my mind here, but I'm quickly learning this is not the place to do it. I paint. I do lots of things."

"What kind of painting?"

"Whatever the moment dictates. Sometimes realism, sometimes cubism, usually shit. I do my best work when I'm drunk. That's the only time I'm really honest with myself."

We reached the lobby, zipped our jackets and pushed through the doors.

"Colder than a well-digger's ass," said Wolf, bracing against the late February wind.

"Or a witch's tit in a brass brassiere."

"That's good. I'll add it to my repertoire."

The campus was frozen and empty. Since an early freeze in October, the land lay dead, cold and barren, unrelieved by a covering of snow.

"What are two smart guys like us doing in a frozen shit hole like this?" asked Wolf.

"I've been asking myself that a lot lately. I'm tired of school, but I keep telling myself to finish the degree. But I wonder sometimes. I'm ready to join the real world. Whatever that is. Why do you hang around?"

"Cowardice. I'd give both balls to transfer to NYU, but the parents say they won't pay for it. And I'm too chicken to try it on my own. They think if they keep me corn-fed in Iowa until I finish college, I'll somehow become a normal son. Little do they know that they're contributing to my insanity. But I rather enjoy being insane."

We reached The Walrus where a barrage of smoke, loud music and stale beer assaulted us when we opened the door.

"The smells and sounds of home," sighed Wolf. We found an empty booth at the back. I was relieved to see a familiar waitress from one of my classes approach for our order. She wouldn't ask for an ID. We ordered beer.

Wolf took a long drink from his bottle. "Ah," he sighed. "The beginning of a sort of peace."

"Have you ever read O'Neill?" I asked after a swallow of beer.

"O'Neill who?" Wolf took another long drink.

"Eugene O'Neill. The playwright. *Long Day's Journey Into Night*, *The Iceman Cometh*, *Strange Interlude*."

"I think I've heard of him, but I try not to clutter my mind with other people's ideas. They obscure what it's all about. What about him? Do you like him?" He drained his bottle. "Ready for another one?"

"You're way ahead of me."

He ordered another beer. "Tell me about this O'Neill."

"Your comments reminded me of him. Some of his characters think alcohol allows them to see through the fog of everyday life to something greater."

"Sounds like my kind of man. With enough booze, the inhibitions and bullshit are gone. Honesty takes over."

"Maybe," I said, doubtfully. "But doesn't alcohol simply create another illusion? Maybe there isn't any truth or reality—not to mention honesty."

"Of course, there isn't. We have to create our realities. I prefer the ones created by booze. Or sex. I'd like to drink myself to death or fuck myself to death. Maybe both. What's your preference?"

"I'm not sure," I said. "I haven't done a lot of either."

"You mean you're a virgin?"

I smiled sheepishly and shrugged.

"What's your preference? Men or women?"

"Women," I said, and then hated the lie.

"I fuck anything," said Wolf. "But I guess my preference is women. That'll surprise everyone on campus. They all think I'm queer."

That was my guess.

Suddenly changing the subject, he asked, "Do you like classical music?"

"I don't know it too well. I like some of it."

"What do you like?"

I thought a moment. "I like Tchaikovsky's 'Romeo and Juliet Overture,' 'La Mer' . . ."

Wolf made a face and interrupted. "Schmaltzy shit! But maybe you'll outgrow it. John Cage is the only one doing anything interesting with music today. Do you know his stuff?"

I said I didn't.

"I have some of his records. I'll play them for you sometime. You need an education, the kind you won't get from the Pablum they feed you at this place. Maybe I'll take you under my wing. You show promise." He drained his second beer. I was only halfway through my first one.

Wolf was the first outrageously nonconforming person I met. He was new on campus and quickly became one of its characters. He wore the same paint-spattered jeans and sweatshirt wherever he went, even Sunday meals in the Commons where coats and ties were expected of male students. For some reason, no one ever challenged him. He had short dark hair when he arrived, but by spring it was shoulder-length. He shaved periodically, but usually his beard was either too short or too long for respectability. His thick, horn rimmed glasses always rode the end of his nose. He smoked constantly and his room was fogged with smoke. Almost every night he was at The Walrus, and when it closed, he invited his drinking buddies back to his room where he kept an illicit stash of booze. He rarely attended classes.

Wolf was from a small city in western Iowa, the only child of well-to-do parents who paid his tuition, room and board and sent him a generous monthly allowance. He saw them once a year at Christmas, apparently a satisfactory arrangement for them all. Two small liberal arts colleges preceded his appearance on campus. He flunked out of one and escaped expulsion from the other for drinking on campus after he promised to leave at the end of the semester. At mid-term, he received notices that he was failing all his classes. His parents received the same notices.

"I heard from mater and pater," he told me one evening at The Walrus. "They're concerned that I'm flunking my classes."

"What'd you tell them?"

"My usual line. No one in this hick place is enlightened enough to understand me. That my kind of people are in New York, and if they'd send me there all would be okay."

"And did they buy it?"

"I think pater's actually considering it. He probably figured it would get me farther away from him. Mater cried, of course."

Two days later, I was returning from the newspaper office and took a short cut through the back courtyard of the dorm. I stopped short. Wolf was dancing naked among the leafless March bushes. He leapt into the air, bowed down, slithered on the ground, and twisted his body through a series of contortions. A small crowd gathered to watch him. It was a chilly day with occasional snowflakes, but Wolf was oblivious to the cold. Finally, he stopped. He noted the small audience for the first time, bowed and put on his robe. He was walking toward the door of the dorm when he spotted me.

"A bit chilly for that sort of thing, isn't it?" I asked, joining him

"I hadn't noticed."

"I didn't know you were a dancer."

"Of course, I am. I'm an artist. Snoopy is right."

"Snoopy?"

"You know, the dog in *Peanuts*."

"I don't get it."

"Don't tell me you don't read *Peanuts*?" he said, exasperated. "It should be required reading instead of the crap they stuff down you here."

We entered the dormitory and walked down the hall toward our rooms. Wolf continued talking. "Snoopy says dance is the only pure art form. And he's right. There's nothing between the artist and his expression, especially if he dances without music. No paint, no canvas, no words, no instruments. And if you dance in the nude, there's absolutely nothing between you and your creation. And if you dance outside, all the better. You and the universe are one."

Several days later, Wolf asked me to stop by his room when I returned from the library. I rapped on his door and was told to enter. He was stripped to his underwear, washing his hands in the basin.

"Be with you in a minute," he said. "Find a place to sit."

That wasn't easy. The room was total chaos, piles on every surface. A canvas was propped near the opened window. I examined it. I never knew what to expect from Wolf's painting. This one was incredibly ugly, splattered browns were brushed into schizophrenic swirls.

"Do you like it?" he asked, pulling on his jeans.

"Not particularly."

"I don't like it either."

"Is it called something?"

"I call it 'Humanity.' I shit on the canvas, pissed on it, spit at it and mixed it up."

"Jesus, Wolf! That's disgusting!"

"'Disgusting,'" he mused. "That's a good name for it, too. Same difference." He grabbed his jacket. "Let's go eat. Better yet, let's forget eating and go get drunk."

It was late April and spring finally arrived. Warm weather and light rains coaxed blossoms from their buds and turned the campus green. I cut my afternoon classes and spent several hours wandering the campus, finding private places where I removed my shirt and enjoyed the sun's warmth on my bare skin. I returned to the dorm in late afternoon and decided to see what Wolf was up to. I knocked on his door and his voice invited me in.

I opened the door. He was lying on the bed in his underwear, smoking a cigarette and staring at the ceiling. He ignored me. The room was filled with smoke, the window was closed, the draperies pulled.

"Why are you hiding away in this dark, stuffy room on such a beautiful day?"

"Fuck the beautiful day."

"Something wrong?"

"Fuck it!"

"Maybe I better come back anther time."

"Fuck everything!" he screamed. "Fuck! Fuck! Fuck! Fuck! Fuck!"

I left the room. Wolf was still screaming "Fuck!" when I crossed the hall to my room.

In retrospect, I wonder how I made it through that semester. I was burnt-out with college. As liberating as it was intellectually, I felt it was keeping me from experiencing the world beyond Iowa. I seriously considered dropping out and taking off for someplace warm. But the pragmatic Scot in me said persevere for another year when I would have my degree and more options—not to mention Miss Cotters' trust fund.

But I was frustrated. Bored with classes, I found it increasingly difficult to repress my sexuality. I was horny all the time. Some days the campus seemed filled with hunky men and I sat in the library daydreaming about them. At such times in the past, I increased my hours at the newspaper and plunged more deeply into classes and jerked off to quell my horniness. But it wasn't working this time.

I was tired of the newspaper and most of the people who worked there. I had a dull set of professors whose classes were even duller. I did minimal work and coasted on my reputation. Consequently, I had lots of time on my hands, much of which I spent with Wolf. And a good deal of that time was spent at The Walrus drinking beer.

It was mid-May, a Friday. Wolf suggested we go slumming in the small industrial city that neighbored the college. It was early evening when we discovered a grubby bar tucked among warehouses near the railroad tracks. The bartender was talking to a middle-aged woman as worn as his old bar. Three very drunk men dressed in dirty overalls sat at the opposite end. We found a table and ordered a pitcher of beer.

"This is real life," said Wolf. "It beats the hypocrisy and bullshit of the campus. These people live the nitty-gritty. They live life. They don't need to read books to learn about it."

"I suspect you're right about the books," I said, checking out the patrons. "I don't think they read too many."

"You grew up with farmers. Farmers are the noblest people on earth."

"I thought you didn't like the farmers on campus?"

"They're not farmers. They're half-educated assholes.

They should've stayed on their farms. Education corrupts them."

"If farms are so great, why don't you find a farm instead of going to New York City? Christ, New York is the antithesis of a farm."

"I'm not talking about me. I'm talking about normal people, the dull ones. They should stay on farms."

The discussion was going nowhere.

Wolf continued. "Come to New York with me. Let's leave tomorrow. Fuck this stupid college. Fuck Iowa. We can hitchhike and get jobs when we get there. You said you had a great time in New York when you were a kid."

"That was a different New York and a different time. New York City's not my place. Too crowded, too cold. I want some place warm."

Suddenly Wolf announced, "Enough of this place." He poured the remaining beer into his glass and drained it. "On to the next one."

We left the tavern. Wolf drove two blocks, spotted another tavern and parked in front of it. It was crowded with factory workers, but we found an empty table at the back and ordered a pitcher of beer. It was too noisy to talk so we downed the beer and left.

I lost count of the bars we visited as we drank into the night. Wolf drank twice as much as I did, but he had no trouble driving to the next bar. At one of them an old man joined us. He rambled on about a life that I was too drunk to pretend I was interested in. At another, an aging hooker tried to pick me up, but gave up when she realized I was either too drunk or too disinterested, or both. At a noisy bar near a bus station, an old woman told me I had green eyes like her son. Then she started crying because her son was killed at Bataan during the war.

Faces and places blurred. Sometimes we drank with people we picked up. At other times, I found myself drinking alone. Wolf always appeared, however, and dragged me to the next place. I have no idea what we talked about, but it all seemed intense and insightful. At midnight, we were at a Negro dance club. A sea of dark faces moved rhythmically to loud music. We were the only whites in the club and stumbled to the sounds that moved the crowd.

Late in the night, I was in a bar so dark I could hardly see. I was very drunk and bumped into dark figures. I couldn't find Wolf. I leaned against a wall to steady myself. Across the room, a man stared at me, a very attractive man. My eyes focused on him. I wanted that man and I knew he wanted me. I stumbled across the undulating floor and stood beside him. We didn't speak. He touched my cheek and I touched his. He nodded toward the back of the room, turned and walked in that direction. I followed him, bumping into other men and stumbling over chairs. I found him in a small, dimly lighted room. He locked the door. He pulled me to him and embraced me. He unbuckled his belt, unzipped his fly and dropped his pants. I reached down and felt his hard dick. I wanted that dick. I fell to my knees into a swirling sea of darkness.

I woke up mid-afternoon the next day in my bed at the dorm. I was fully dressed. My face and pillow were caked with dried vomit. I turned to get out of bed and barfed on the floor. I stumbled to the basin, turned on the water and continued barfing. When I stopped, I rinsed my mouth and face in cold water. The stench of the room was making me nauseous again. I opened the window, found some towels and wiped off my bed and cleaned up the floor. I stripped my clothes and put on a robe. I went into the hall, walked to the laundry room and shoved my barfy clothes, towels and sheets into a washer. I showered for an eternity, occasionally retching with dry heaves.

My head was still pounding when I returned to my room. I tried to remember the night before, but only recalled blurred images. Then I remembered the man in the dark room. I saw his face distinctly. I remembered the feel of his hard dick. I wanted that man. And if I hadn't passed out I would've had him. Despite my aching head and churning stomach, a warm pleasure crept through me when I thought of the man in the dark room.

I spent the rest of the afternoon in bed. My head throbbed and my stomach churned, but I didn't throw up again. The room was darkening into evening when someone knocked on the door.

"Come in," I said.

"The dead's alive." It was Wolf. He entered and closed the door. "I stopped by twice but you were sleeping. I brought you some sustenance." He placed crackers and tomato juice on the desk.

"Thanks. I feel terrible. How are you?"

"Terrible this morning, but I'm okay now. You were really out of it last night."

"Tell me. Where were we when I passed out?"

"I've no idea. Some guy told me you passed out in the

backroom. I found you on the floor. He helped me get you to the car. I don't even remember driving back here. I probably couldn't find any of those places we hit last night. How about you?"

"It's all fuzzy. Jesus, why'd we drink so much? We were crazy."

"Isn't it great being crazy?" Suddenly he jumped up. "Fuck! I forgot the big news. That's why I stopped by. I'm going to New York! Pater called today and told me he's decided to foot my bill in New York City for six months to see if I can make it."

"That's great. What changed his mind?"

"Who knows? Who cares? At last I'm free of these cornfields!"

"When do you go?"

"Any time. I'm flunking all my classes, so there's no need to linger. I think I'll celebrate at The Walrus with a hair of the dog. Care to join me?"

"Jesus, no! The thought of a drink makes me want to barf!"

"New York!" shouted Wolf. He jumped and tried to click his heels together but slipped on the rug. "Fuck! I'm out of here!"

The next day I stopped by Wolf's room. No one responded to my knock. I turned the knob and opened the door. The room was its usual chaos, but scrawled on a wall was "Goodbye, fuck heads! New York, here I come!"

Midway through the summer back in Tools Rock, I received a letter postmarked New York City with no return address. Inside was an unsigned note: "I am at peace."

Gunnar

I MET GUNNAR BRANNAN the fall of my senior year. Several years earlier, he dropped out of school for unclear reasons. Now he was back on campus. He was a couple years older than I and a couple inches taller with black hair, dark brown eyes and a strong athletic body. He was a very good-looking man in an unorthodox way. At least I thought so.

It was a busy semester. I was taking a full load of classes and editing the newspaper with Es. One of my classes was "Chaucer" taught by my favorite professor, an eccentric middle aged woman who raised burros and looked like she coiffed her hair each morning with an egg beater. Only eight students signed-up for the class, most of them the regulars I came to expect in my upper division courses. As we waited for the professor on the first day, Gunnar appeared at the door. I assumed he had the wrong room.

"Is this the Chaucer class?" he asked.

Someone told him it was and he took a seat. A few minutes later, the professor arrived with her tangled hair askew and announced she would keep us only long enough to explain the syllabus. She soon became caught up in Chaucer's England, however, and held us five minutes beyond the bell.

Each day when Gunnar arrived for class, he nodded to me and sat a couple seats away. He took voluminous notes and asked good questions. I was impressed by him.

Late one Thursday night after the newspaper was put to bed, Es and I stopped by The Walrus for beer and pizza. A late-breaking story and a temperamental linotype machine made it a difficult edition. We were hungry and exhausted.

The Walrus was almost empty. We found a booth away from the noisy jukebox and rehashed the paper. A waiter arrived for our order. I looked up and was surprised to see Gunnar.

"Hi," I said. "I didn't know you worked here."

"Yeah. Quite a change from Chaucer, eh?"

"I think he would approve. Es, this is Gunnar Brannan from my Chaucer class. Gunnar meet Es Stevens."

They acknowledged one another and I gave our order. Gunnar brought a pitcher of beer which we seriously dented while awaiting the pizza that arrived some minutes later. Conversation slowed as we devoured the pizza. Gunnar removed the empty platter and replenished our beer.

I noticed him sitting alone at the bar and asked Es, "Do you mind if I call Gunnar over? He looks bored"

"Sure, invite him over."

GUNNAR

I caught Gunnar's attention and he approached us.

"Are you allowed to socialize with customers?" I asked.

"Sure thing," he replied with a big smile. "I'm here to keep our customers happy."

"Care to join us?"

"Thanks. I'll get a Coke. No beer on the job." He returned with a Coke and sat beside Es.

"How do you like the Chaucer class?" I asked.

"Love it. Woods is a bit chaotic at times, but I like her. She certainly knows her material, doesn't she?"

"She certainly does. I think we're in a minority though. Her disorganization turns most students off. I didn't know you were a lit major."

"I'm not. I'm a history major. Chaucer's an elective."

"I heard you were a physics major."

"I was. But no more. I saw the light."

"Not entirely," I said, "or you'd be a lit major."

He smiled and said, "I'm still working on it. At this point I'm interested in so many things I can't settle down to one major. I wish this had happened when I was a freshman."

"Better late than never," said Es, unoriginally.

"Yeah, I guess so," agreed Gunnar. "Sometimes I feel like an illiterate in that Chaucer class. The rest of you have much more lit under your belts."

"You don't sound like an illiterate. You keep the class going at times."

"You don't do so bad." He smiled at me and our eyes momentarily connected. The door opened and five noisy students burst into the barroom.

"Duty calls," said Gunnar. "It was nice talking to you. Good meeting you, Es. See you in class, Lach." He greeted the new arrivals.

Es and I finished our beer and called it a night.

The following Tuesday, I returned to the dorm late. I slipped a story that needed rewriting under the sports editor's door and walked down the hall toward my room. As I passed the shower room, Gunnar stepped into the hall wearing only a towel. We collided and in the ensuing shuffle, his towel fell off.

"Sorry about that," I said, picking up my books and papers as Gunnar picked up his towel. I caught a quick glimpse of his respectable endowment.

"My fault," said Gunnar. He replaced his towel and helped me pick up my papers. "How's your Chaucer paper coming?"

"I haven't got a topic yet. How about you?"

"I'm thinking of doing something with 'The Nun's Priest's Tale.' I'm talking to Woods about it tomorrow."

"You're way ahead of me." My eyes dropped to the bulge under Gunnar's towel.

He looked at me steadily. "I gotta be. I'm a little slow in that class. Wanna come to my room and talk?"

"Sure. We won't bother your roommate?"

"I have a single."

"Me too." We walked down the hall.

Gunnar opened his door. A single bed, an easy chair, a chest of drawers and a desk furnished the little room. A wash basin filled one corner. Books covered every surface and much of the floor.

"Sit here." He moved books from the chair.

"You have a lot of books," I said, sitting down.

"Yeah. That's where my money goes."

"Same here. I love books. I can't bear parting with them after I read them."

"Me too." He removed papers and more books from his bed and sat with his back against the wall, his legs stretched and crossed in front of him. "I suppose the time comes when you run out of space. I've almost reached that time."

"Why did you leave physics?" I asked.

"I really became disillusioned with school. I got bored with physics and decided to take a break."

"What did you do?"

He shrugged. "Worked here and there. Hitchhiked to the East Coast and back."

"Sounds great. Did you like it?"

"At first. It was great seeing all those places, but I soon realized I had to go back to school, that there's a lot I need to learn."

"I can hardly wait to travel. After I finish school I'm taking off."

"Where you going?" He slipped his hand to his crotch and casually adjusted it to a more comfortable position. He looked up and saw me watching him.

"Everywhere. You name it." I raised my eyes to his.

After several moments of silence, he said, "You're an interesting fellow."

"So are you."

We looked at one another quietly. Gunnar eased from

the bed, his towel bulging from his erection, and stood beside me.

Blood pounded through my head. His erection was at my eye level. My dick was about to burst through my jeans. I looked up at him. He squatted beside me. Our faces were inches apart. He put his hand behind my head and pulled me closer. Our lips met. He dropped his towel and urged me toward the bed. I tore off my clothes and we locked in a tight embrace, our mouths consuming and our hands exploring. I'll spare the details, but suffice it to say it was the sexual encounter I'd fantasized for years. I was blown away by a passion and pleasure I never knew existed.

After we were spent, Gunnar settled into a sitting position and said, "I've wanted to do that since I first saw you."

"I've wanted to do that all my life, but I hadn't met you yet."

"You mean this is your first time?"

"My very first time."

"Welcome to the club."

I floated through the next few weeks. Gunnar and I were inseparable. On nights when I worked late at the office, I hurried back to the dorm where Gunnar was waiting. We ripped off our clothes, devoured one another's bodies and fell asleep entwined. Before dawn, I slipped back to my room, almost hoping someone would see me so the campus would know about me and Gunnar. On nights when he worked at The Walrus, I waited up for him. Shortly after midnight, he tapped lightly on the door with pizza and beer. Sometimes we consumed the pizza and beer first, but usually we made love and talked until dawn, eating the cold pizza and drinking the warm beer.

I babbled about Gunnar to everyone at the newspaper. They thought he was simply a new friend, but Es suspected otherwise.

One weekend, Gunnar went home to visit his mother who was recovering from surgery. It was the first time we were separated since we met. I was moping in the newspaper offices on Saturday morning. Es was in her office next door.

"I thought you'd be out with Gunnar today," she said, standing in the door smoking a cigarette.

"He's gone home for the weekend."

"Good. Maybe I'll get a chance to spend some time with you. You like him a lot don't you?"

I looked at her steadily and said, "It's more than that, Es. I'm in love with him."

She was quiet momentarily and then said, "I suspected that." She took a long drag on her cigarette.

"You did? Do the others know?"

"I doubt it. They think he's just a friend."

"You can tell them if you want to. I want everyone to know. I'm a homosexual, you know."

"Do tell?" she said, blowing smoke through her nose. "You don't have to be a whiz kid to figure that one out."

"You mean everyone knows?" I asked, somewhat apprehensively.

"Of course not. Why would they? I've always known. I pick up on things like that. And I keep my friends' secrets secret."

"I don't care if they know."

"I wouldn't broadcast it if I were you. It's not a way to win popularity contests."

"Who cares? They'll soon figure it out anyway."

"Be careful, Lach. You could get kicked out of school, you know."

"For loving Gunnar?"

"I'm afraid so."

I was quiet. I knew she was right. That's why we slipped through the halls at night to see one another. That's why the books about homosexuality were restricted at the library.

"Don't do anything crazy, Lach. Infatuations make people do dumb things."

I was offended. "This isn't infatuation. I'm in love with Gunnar."

"I'm just telling you to be careful."

"Lach! Wake up!"

I opened my eyes and looked at the clock. It was 7:30. Someone was pounding on my door. I rolled out of bed and opened the door. It was Gunnar.

"Why are you up so early?" I stood back and let him in.

"We're going to the Mississippi to see the fall colors. I heard they're spectacular. We'll stay overnight somewhere and come back tomorrow."

"What about classes and the newspaper?"

"Nothing's happening in classes and Es can cover you at the paper. C'mon and get dressed."

"Let me think a minute."

"Don't think. Just do it. I filled the car with gas."

"You're crazy. It's Tuesday. Why not wait until the weekend?"

"There'll be too many people out. Besides, I have to work this weekend. C'mon. You don't need anything."

I shrugged, "Okay." I dressed, went down the hall to the telephone and woke a sleepy Es who said she would cover for me. Ten minutes later we left campus.

We drove northeast toward the wooded hills of the Mississippi River. Clusters of colored trees dotted the rolling farmlands. We stopped in a tiny town at noon for sandwiches and picked up a map at a service station where we got directions to a highway that meandered along the bluffs of the Mississippi. As we neared the river, hills became more pronounced and woods more extensive. A steel-gray sky exuded melancholy over the countryside, but the brilliant wooded hills exploded colors into the day. We found a motel on a bluff overlooking the river.

"We can't afford this place," I said, as Gunnar pulled off the highway.

"Sure we can." He stopped the car and went into the motel office. A few minutes later, he returned with keys and a big grin. "We got the best one."

"How much?"

"Five bucks."

"Five bucks! How'd you do that?"

"I told her we're students and don't have much money. She gave me the best cabin for the lowest off season rate." He drove to the farthest cabin. We went inside and Gunnar flopped on the bed while I explored the kitchen.

"C'mere," he called. "I got something for you."
I returned to the bedroom. He had undone his pants and was waving his erection at me.

"I got something for you, too," I said, jumping on him and pinning him down. He flipped me over and our wrestling match evolved into a passionate bout of sex. Afterwards we went outdoors and watched the river traffic slide by the late afternoon colors on the opposite bank.

"I sometimes forget all this beauty is out here when I'm caught up in campus life," Gunnar mused.

"Same here. Each fall I'm amazed at the spectacular colors. Fall is death and dying, but yet it's so beautiful. Maybe that's the way death really is, not the gloomy, sad way we usually depict it."

Gunnar smiled at me quietly and said, "You're a poet."
I smiled back. "And you're my muse."

At dusk we drove into a nearby small town and found a restaurant operated by two middle-aged sisters who served home-cooked meals. After eating, we explored the town and then drove back to our cabin. We built a fire in the fireplace and lay in front of it, propped on pillows.

"What are your plans after graduation?" I asked.

"I'm seriously thinking about grad school. I'm just beginning to learn. How about you?"

"I'm considering grad school too."

"English?"

"I don't think so," I said. "I'm really attracted to anthropology. I've been reading a lot of it. I wish they offered classes here."

"I don't know much about it. That's Margaret Mead, isn't it?"

"Yeah, among other things. It pulls together a lot of stuff I'm interested in. Like American Indians. Anthropologists write most of the stuff about Indians. Ancient civilizations. Languages. Evolution and ape-men. I really find that stuff fascinating."

"My problem is I find everything fascinating. I'm not sure I want to continue in history."

"We should do grad work at the same school."

"Yeah," said Gunnar. "Meanwhile, let's go to bed. I got some other kind of work in mind for tonight."

We made-out into the late night, slept, and then made-out some more. It was almost noon when we left the cabin. We had lunch at the same restaurant where we ate the previous night and then began the drive home. A light rain fell and by the time we reached campus it was a heavy downpour. We parked the car and ran through the rain to the dorm.

Inside, I said, "Thanks, Gun. It was really special."

He winked at me. "You better believe it. See you tomorrow."

Thanksgiving was a couple weeks away. One evening after a bout of sex, I asked Gunnar about his plans for the holiday.

"Didn't I tell you? I'm going to Illinois to see my girlfriend."

I was taken aback. "Your girlfriend?"

"Yeah. Susan. She goes to Wilmer College outside Chicago. Haven't I told you about her?"

"No, you haven't. Is this a real girlfriend?"

"I guess she's pretty real. We plan to get married after we graduate. I want you to meet her someday. I think you'd like one another. I gotta go." He began dressing. "I need some sleep before that exam tomorrow."

I quietly watched him dress.

"Take care." He kissed me and left the room.

I was stunned. I couldn't sleep. I'd never discussed it with Gunnar, but I assumed we'd finish school, find someplace to live and always be together. He'd never said so, but I thought that's what he had in mind too. But he was getting married. And not to me.

I isolated myself in my room the next day. I called the newspaper and told Es I had the flu and wouldn't be in. That night shortly after midnight, Gunnar tapped on my door, but I didn't answer. He saw me in the hallway the next day and asked where I was the previous night. I told him I worked late. When he suggested we meet that evening, I said I was coming down with the flu. On the third day, I decided to confront him.

Gunnar worked that night. When he returned to the dorm, he knocked on my door and I let him in. He placed the pizza and beer on the desk and pulled me to him.

"I'm really hungry," I said. "Let's eat first."

"I'm hungry, too." He groped me. "But whatever you say." He unboxed the pizza and opened two bottles of beer. "Are you feeling better?"

"I wasn't sick."

"What was wrong?"

"You don't know?"

"Should I?"

"I sort of hoped you might." I paused. "I didn't know you had a girlfriend. I didn't know you were going to get married."

He looked puzzled. "What difference does that make?"

"What difference does that make? Jesus, Gunnar! I thought we had something going."

"We do. At least I thought we did. You could've fooled me."

"God damn it, Gunnar. I love you. I don't want you to have a girlfriend. I don't want you to get married. I want you to be with me."

"Jesus, Lach." He paused. "That's not the way it works."

"Then we're going to change the way it works. I love you, Gun. I thought we'd be together a long time. Maybe the rest of our lives."

"Come on, Lach. Normal men don't do that. That's queer."

"We're not normal men, Gunnar. We're queers."

He stiffened and put his beer down. "Speak for yourself, Lach. A little hanky-panky with you doesn't make me a queer."

"You're queer, Gunnar. Men don't suck other men's dicks unless they're queer."

"C'mon, Lach. You're making a big deal out of this." He started to undo his pants.

"Take your fucking pizza and beer and get out of here."

"Get real, Lach. It doesn't work that way."

"Maybe not here. But somewhere there's a place where it works that way. And I'm going to find it."

"Jesus," he said, exasperated. He grabbed his jacket and left.

I made it through the week and managed to get the paper out on time with a good deal of help from Es. She realized something was wrong and several times asked me what was happening. I initially denied anything was wrong, but eventually told her I wasn't seeing Gunnar anymore and didn't want to talk about it.

It was Friday night. Normally, I'd be in my room anticipating Gunnar's arrival. But I decided I wouldn't see him again. He'd come to my door twice, but I didn't let him in. The night before, I told him to never come back and he left angry.

I felt used and betrayed. I walked across campus, not sure where I was going. Snowflakes began falling, but even the delicate first flakes of the season couldn't penetrate my dark mood. I decided to go to the newspaper offices. It was late and hopefully no one would be around. I entered the building and climbed the creaky stairs to the third floor. I looked at the worn wooden treads, wondering if others had climbed the stairs hurting with the same hurt that welled within me. I inserted the key in my office door and noticed a light in Es' office across the hall. I sat at my desk in the darkness and absently stared out the window, watching the thickening snow quietly lighten the dark night.

Es' door opened. She stood in my doorway, smoking her usual cigarette, also watching the falling snow. After several moments of silence, she said, "How about a stroll in the snow?"

GUNNAR

I didn't answer immediately and then said, "Okay."

We quietly put on our coats. Es slung a huge yellow purse over her shoulder and we walked down the stairs into the snowy night. She slipped her arm through mine and we let the sidewalk dictate our direction. The campanile chimed nine when we passed beneath it. The snow was falling rapidly, sticking to everything, and the campus was becoming homogenized in white. We didn't speak. The sidewalk took us to the empty football field. We walked its length in silence. When we retraced our steps, our footprints were already obliterated by the snow. We again passed the campanile where a small wind whipped up a whirlwind of white. It subsided and we stopped, watching the campus become a snowscape of white trees, white benches, white buildings, white sidewalks and white lawns. We sat on a bench, the snowflakes blending us into the white night. Only the black sky and the lights of the streetlamps were not white. We continued our silence.

Finally Es said, "I'm sorry, Lach."

The campanile began striking again, its peals muffled by the soft snowy night. When it concluded, I said, "I know. Me too."

We watched the snow for several more moments. I felt it clinging to my eyelashes.

"How about a hot chocolate?" suggested Es. "My treat."

"Sounds like a winner."

We stood. Es gave me a long hug. I hugged her back. We walked arm in arm through the snow to the student union and the hot chocolate.

Summer

I STEPPED FROM THE shower, began drying and joined the Andrews Sisters in "Bounce Me Brother with a Solid Four." I tossed the towel on the bed and saw my reflection in the full-length mirror. I stopped singing and turned off the record player. I walked to the mirror and stood before it appraisingly.

Green eyes looked back at me. My damp hair was a tangle of dark curls and white even teeth showed through my lips. Strong arms hung at my sides. My nipples protruded through the black hair that dusted my chest. The hair narrowed into a thin line down my tight belly and sprayed out again into a dense dark triangle at my crotch. The head of my dick peeked through my foreskin and my balls hung heavily. The hair thinned again over my thighs and continued down my calves. Solid feet supported me.

I never thought much about my looks. I looked in the mirror every day of my life and saw the same me. No big deal. For twenty-two years, I'd been looking at that face and that body. It was me and that was that. But today I looked different. I decided I looked pretty damn good.

SUMMER

"Lach!" Mom called from downstairs. "Hurry up. We'll be late."

"Okay, Mom. I'll be right down."

A month earlier, I graduated with honors and college was already a closed chapter in my life. Miss Cotters' trust fund was transferred to me and I gave a thousand dollars each to Mom, Dad, Duncan and Maggie. The balance would pay for my trip and anything left would go toward graduate studies in anthropology. In three hours, I would board a plane for my first plane ride, the first leg of a journey that would take me around the world in a year or maybe two.

I continued studying myself in the mirror. Years ago Letha told me I was different. She must've known when I was just a little kid. And good old Pine Camp, thanks for letting me know there's a world out there filled with diversity, adventure and excitement. Miss Cotters, this trip is especially for you. Yesterday I carved our names on the big red rock in the Square, and now you and I are going to see the world! Maybe I'll run into you, Grant, if you're still around somewhere. And maybe I'll catch up with you in California, Ross. I hope so. Thanks for introducing me to all those wonderful books, Mr. Fraser. And all you professors and your great classes and that beautiful library, thanks for the prep work. Wolf, you're absolutely right; it's incredibly dull to be normal. But Gunnar, you're dead wrong. Somewhere out there's a place where it's okay for men to love one another and I'm going to find it. And Tools Rock, I'm leaving you like I always said I would. But I'll be back, damn you! Like it or not, you're a big part of me and I'll always come home to you.

"Lach!" Mom called again. "We must leave if we're going to get to the airport on time. We'll wait for you in the car."

"I'm on my way, Mom."

I looked again at myself in the mirror, broke into a big grin and winked at my image. I grabbed my crotch with both hands, leaned back and howled, "Whoopee!" I pulled on my clothes, picked up my suitcase and clattered down the stairs. I opened the front door and yelled as loud as I could, "Here I come!"

Also by H. Arlo Nimmo

The Sea People of Sulu

Bajau of the Philippines

The Pele Literature

The Songs of Salanda

Magosaha

The Andrews Sisters

*Good and Bad Times in a
San Francisco Neighborhood*

Pele, Volcano Goddess of Hawai'i

A Very Far Place

Made in the USA
San Bernardino, CA
05 February 2014